SPECIAL MESSAGE TO READERS

This book is published under the auspices of

THE ULVERSCROFT FOUNDATION

(registered charity No. 264873 UK)

Established in 1972 to provide funds for research, diagnosis and treatment of eye diseases. Examples of contributions made are: —

A Children's Assessment Unit at Moorfield's Hospital, London.

•

Twin operating theatres at the Western Ophthalmic Hospital, London.

•

A Chair of Ophthalmology at the Royal Australian College of Ophthalmologists.

•

The Ulverscroft Children's Eye Unit at the Great Ormond Street Hospital For Sick Children, London.

You can help further the work of the Foundation by making a donation or leaving a legacy. Every contribution, no matter how small, is received with gratitude. Please write for details to:

THE ULVERSCROFT FOUNDATION,
The Green, Bradgate Road, Anstey,
Leicester LE7 7FU, England.
Telephone: (0116) 236 4325

In Australia write to:
THE ULVERSCROFT FOUNDATION,
c/o The Royal Australian and New Zealand
College of Ophthalmologists,
94-98 Chalmers Street, Surry Hills,
N.S.W. 2010, Australia

BORDER FURY

Buck Starrett, fast-shooting Texas Ranger, is reputed for his determination to win against overwhelming odds. He takes a novice ranger to Adobe Flat on the Mexican border, unaware that he faces his toughest challenge yet. Plunged into an all-out war with Mexican rustlers operating on both sides of the border, Starrett must also shoot his way into the crooked situation enveloping Adobe Flat to overcome the criminal element — then shoot his way out again.

CORBA SUNMAN

BORDER FURY

Complete and Unabridged

LINFORD
Leicester

First published in Great Britain in 2010 by
Robert Hale Limited
London

First Linford Edition
published 2011
by arrangement with
Robert Hale Limited
London

British Library CIP Data

Sunman, Corba.
  Border fury. - - (Linford western library)
  1. Western stories.
  2. Large type books.
  I. Title II. Series
  823.9'2–dc22

ISBN 978–1–44480–514–7

Published by
F. A. Thorpe (Publishing)
Anstey, Leicestershire

Set by Words & Graphics Ltd.
Anstey, Leicestershire
Printed and bound in Great Britain by
T. J. International Ltd., Padstow, Cornwall

1

The two riders had followed the winding trail for over a week, heading into the great south-west of Texas, and in that time they had learned all there was to know about each other. Now they had reached a fork in the trail and Buck Starrett, a veteran Texas Ranger of five years, had to follow the fork due south to Denville while Del Baker, a novice embarking on his first law job, was going on to Adobe Flat on the Mexican/Texas border to set up an investigation into large scale rustling.

They reined in at the fork. Starrett stepped down from his bay and stretched to get the kinks out of his back and neck. They had ridden fifteen miles since dawn; Starrett stretched his arms wide, threw back his head, and flexed his powerful muscles. He was a big man in every way; tall, heavily built, his broad frame rippling with muscle. He took off his black Stetson, cuffed sweat from his rugged forehead, and then replaced the hat, pulling the brim low over his brown eyes. He dropped his right hand to the butt of his pistol, drew the weapon and blew dust from its mechanism.

Baker remained in his saddle. He was tall and lean, with blond hair and blue eyes; he was five years younger than Starrett. The instructions given him by Ranger Captain Ben Ketchell had been simple.

'I ain't throwing you in at the deep end, Baker,' Captain Ketchell had said. 'You're going along mainly for the experience. Buck will boss the investigation and you just do like he tells you. It's unfortunate that a murder has come up in Denville, but Buck will soon get the killer, and then he'll join you in Adobe Flat and you'll start in on the main chore. While Buck is in Denville I want you to ride into the Circle B ranch west of Adobe Flat,

2

which is owned by Toke Bellamy, an old saddle pard of mine. Toke was a Ranger thirty years ago, and he's written me saying he's got urgent problems and needs help damn quick. Now when Toke starts calling for help then you can be sure he's way up past his neck in trouble. He'll set you right about what's been happening, and you just mark time down there until Buck arrives. Is that plain or ain't it?'

'Are you straight on your orders, Del?' Starrett asked, checking his cinch.

'Sure, Buck, and I'm raring to go. I'll have the whole business checked out by the time you show up.'

'Just take it easy,' Starrett warned, his brown eyes filling with concern at the excitement sounding in Baker's voice. 'Remember that you're just riding in to let Bellamy know the law is backing him. Wait until I show up before sticking your nose into anything.'

'Yeah, I know.' Baker grinned and nodded. 'Are you sure you don't want any help to catch that killer in Denville?'

'There is only one killer, so one man can handle it,' Starrett replied, and considered his own orders from Captain Ketchell. The killer, Luke Ardle had set up as a gambler in a saloon in Denville owned by Matt Jefford, and from the start he had run crooked games. His career came to an abrupt end when he was accused of cheating and his protests turned into gun play. When the gunsmoke cleared three men lay dead in the sawdust, but Ardle was not one of them. He had escaped in the ensuing confusion, taking with him the contents of Jefford's safe. The local sheriff, Tom Self, had asked for help in apprehending Ardle, and Starrett had been sidetracked to handle the chore.

'So I'd better split the breeze to Adobe Flat,' Baker remarked. He shook his reins and touched a forefinger to the brim of his Stetson in a farewell salute. 'See you on the border, Buck.'

'And don't forget to take that law badge off your shirt before you report to Bellamy,' Starrett warned. 'We're gonna play it real careful down there until we get to know something about Bellamy's problems. You're gonna take a riding job at the Circle B and act like a cowpuncher until I show up.'

'Heck, I joined the law to get away from ranch work,' Baker protested, his blue eyes glinting.

Starrett watched Baker ride off, and experienced a pang of uneasiness about a newcomer to the grim work of law enforcement being sent in alone. The fact the captain had decided to send two men indicated that the chore was considered to be more difficult than usual, and it was in Starrett's mind to countermand the orders Baker had been given and take the youngster with him to Denville. But he remained motionless, watching Baker's progress until the young lawman had topped a ridge and disappeared into the vast wilderness that stretched all the way to the Mexican border; into an area known locally as the Devil's Outpost.

Starrett looked ahead, facing south.

Denville lay twenty miles off the main trail and there was no way he could reach the isolated town until the next day. He pushed on resolutely, his dark eyes narrowed against the glare of the sun. The scenery changed but little as he progressed and at nightfall he camped in solitary state. The next morning he rode on, and sighted Denville just before noon.

The town seemed to rise up out of the undulating ground, and proved to be just two rows of ugly adobe buildings facing each other across a wide expanse of rutted dust. There was little to show that the town was inhabited. A saddle horse was standing in front of a saloon, its reins wrapped around a hitch rail. There was a buckboard outside the general store, and a youth wearing a dirty white apron was loading supplies into it. A couple of loafers were seated on chairs on the porch of the dusty hotel, their Stetsons tipped forward over their eyes. A board with the faded legend SHERIFF on it in peeling black paint caught Starrett's eye. He nudged his horse towards it and stepped down into the dust.

The door of the law office was standing open and Starrett entered. An old man was seated on a chair behind a battered desk, his elbows resting on the desk and his chin cupped in his gnarled hands. He was snoring gently. Starrett regarded him for a moment, shaking his head. There was a deputy's law star pinned to the oldster's blue shirt. Starrett gently kicked the side of the desk and the old man opened his eyes. He stared at Starrett without moving, then spotted the Ranger badge on Starrett's shirt and sprang to his feet so fast he overturned his chair.

'Gold-durn it,' the oldster said. 'Nothing ever happens around here during siesta so I try to catch up on my sleep; and you walk in and catch me napping. Are you the man the sheriff is waiting for?'

'Very likely,' Starrett replied. 'You had a murder here recently. A gambler by the name of Ardle shot three men.'

'That's right. After the shooting, Ardle high-tailed it out of town with four thousand dollars outa Matt Jefford's safe and stole Jefford's racing horse. A posse went out after him but he got away. The sheriff reckons he ain't left the county. Ardle made some friends while he was around, and maybe they are hiding him. His tracks just disappeared out by Tolliver's ranch and the posse never did find them again.'

'Where is the sheriff? I need to talk to him. I want a description of Ardle and the location of Tolliver's ranch. Maybe one of the men who rode with the posse after Ardle can ride with me to go over the ground and bring me up to date.'

'I'll fetch the sheriff if you'll gimme a minute. He's talked of nothing but meeting you since the day Ardle disappeared.' The oldster limped from behind the desk and headed for the door. 'I won't be five minutes,' he said, and departed.

Starrett walked to the door and stood

looking around the street. He watched the deputy enter the saloon, to emerge moments later followed by a short, fleshy man wearing blue store-bought suit pants and a short-sleeved grey shirt with a law star pinned to it. A gun belt containing a pistol sagged around the sheriff's paunch. They came toward the office at a run.

'I'm Tom Self.' The sheriff held out his hand as he introduced himself,

'Buck Starrett. I need to get moving.' Starrett explained what he wanted. 'I've got another chore along the border so I don't have much time.'

The sheriff nodded and sent the deputy to fetch someone who had ridden with the posse.

'Ike Shadde is the man to ride with you. He knows as much about Ardle as anyone around here. Give him about ten minutes and he'll be ready to ride.'

'OK. I'll get some supplies from the store and come back in ten minutes.'

'It's been more than a week since Ardle disappeared,' the sheriff observed.

'His trail — what there is of it — is cold now.'

'Sure. I'll take a look around. If I don't find any sign of Ardle I'll probably go on to the border and handle that chore before I come back to catch your killer.'

The sheriff grimaced but said nothing. Starrett went along the street to the store. Ten minutes later he returned to the law office, tied a sack of supplies behind his cantle, and inspected the tall, thin man who was waiting with the sheriff inside the office.

Ike Shadde spat a stream of tobacco juice into the street and nodded curtly when the sheriff introduced him.

'Ike is the best tracker in the county,' the old lawman said proudly. 'He's so good he could track a fish through muddy water.'

'But I couldn't find hide or hair of Ardle after his tracks vanished,' Shadde said in a dry-as-dust voice. 'He made a real good job of blotting his sign, and it must have taken him days because I rode a wide circle around the Tolliver place and came up with a great fat zero. You'll be wasting your time covering old ground, Ranger, but I'll go along with you if you've a mind to check it out.'

'I want to do that,' Starrett said firmly. 'Are you ready to ride?'

'Just got to get my horse from the livery barn,' Shadde told him.

'I'll see you outside the livery barn,' Starrett called, and saw Shadde's jaws champing methodically on a quid of tobacco as the man headed off along the street.

Starrett took his leave of the sheriff and rode along to the stable. By the time his bay had drunk its fill at the water trough Ike Shadde was emerging from the ramshackle building leading a roan that had obviously seen better days. They mounted and rode out. Shadde led the way, answering Starrett's questions curtly.

'You knew Ardle pretty well, I guess?' Starrett said.

11

'No. I ain't a gambling man.'

'But you saw him around, huh? What does he look like?'

'Ornery! Got dark hair well greased. Shifty brown eyes. Ain't the kind of man you would trust in any situation. There is something wrong with his left eye. He can't blink with it, and the lid is always halfway down. They called him Dead-eye. But he was real quick on the draw, and never missed with a shot.'

'How far out of town did you lose his tracks?'

'Just past Tolliver's place, which is twelve miles out. It was a real good piece of trail blotting as I ever saw. If you've got the time I reckon we could find which way Ardle went, but it would take a week, I'm guessing.'

'I'll decide when I've had a look around,' Starrett said.

They rode steadily. Southern Texas was a bleak, inhospitable land. A heat haze shimmered in the distance. Low, brushy hills some ten miles ahead broke the seemingly never-ending flatness of the wild country. Starrett realized that his bay was getting tired but he wanted to bring about a quick conclusion to this grim hunt, and he was a lean, hard man with a single-minded attitude toward his grim duty. He suffered the travail of riding through the wilderness with no regard to the discomfort.

The heat of the blazing mid-afternoon sun made Starrett think of a deliciously cool glass of beer but he thrust aside the desire and reached for his canteen. He swigged a mouthful of warm, metallic-tasting water, rolled it around his mouth, and then spat it out. The bay twitched its ears and Starrett patted the animal's neck, reined in and dismounted. He poured a quantity of water into his Stetson and let the horse drink. Shadde waited patiently while silence pressed in around them like a shroud.

The trail seemed never-ending, but Starrett hunched his shoulders and leaned forward in the saddle, his narrowed eyes watching the dusty ground for the faint marks which Shadde assured him was all that was left of Ardle's trail.

Shadows were long on the ground by the time they neared the hills that had been beckoning them ever since they left Denville. The brush thickened as the ground inclined, grew taller, and Shadde took the lead, following a faint trail that was marked by the prints of Ardle's horse. Shadde slowed his pace still more as the brush grew thicker, and Starrett was surprised when Shadde suddenly uttered a yell and vacated his saddle in a swift dive to his right. Starrett heard a horse whinny somewhere ahead as he slid out of his saddle.

The flat crack of a rifle shot sent a series of diminishing echoes across the silent range. Starrett heard the crackle of a slug passing the nape of his neck as he hunted cover. He landed on his right shoulder and rolled in the brush, his right hand snaking his pistol out of its holster. The last of the echoes was grumbling away into the distance as he arose to one knee and peered around, the muzzle of his pistol lifting. He could hear a horse crashing through the brush, and caught a fleeting glimpse of the animal as it passed across a patch that was bare of vegetation. He had barely time to register that the horse was a sorrel before it vanished.

Four more shots rang out, bracketing their position, and gun smoke drifted. Starrett dropped flat until the storm of lead ceased. He was untouched by the slugs and waited for the inevitable follow-up. Shadde was getting cautiously to his knees, his pistol gripped in his right hand. Starrett heard the sound of a horse somewhere ahead departing noisily through the brush, and pushed himself to his feet. He saw his bay standing close by with trailing reins. Shadde's horse was down in the brush — breathing its last. Shadde was cursing silently as he reloaded the spent chambers in his pistol.

'Did you get a look at whoever it was?' Starrett demanded.

'No. But it was a good thing I heard his horse whinny. I hit the dirt before he got off his first shot. He's done for my horse though. It's lucky we ain't far from Tolliver's place.'

'I got a look at his horse — a sorrel. Do you reckon it was Ardle?'

'I'll tell you what I think when I've had a chance to check his tracks,' Shadde replied. 'Ardle stole Jefford's sorrel when he lit out after the murders, so it looks like we're on the right track. It is getting too dark to look for sign now, so I reckon we better pull back, circle, and go on to Tolliver's place for the night. If it was Ardle doing the shooting then he is probably staying with Tolliver, which is what I suspected in the first place.'

'We'd better go in on foot,' Starrett observed.

'It sure looks like I'll have to! That damn Ardle has killed my horse. But the brush peters out just ahead. We can move around and sneak up on Tolliver — see what's doing at his place.'

16

Starrett checked his horse for injury and he was relieved to find the bay unhurt. The sounds of the ambusher's departure had faded quickly and an uneasy silence covered the wilderness. Starrett holstered his pistol and followed Shadde as the tracker went on through the close vegetation.

The increasing shadows of night began cutting down their range of vision, and Starrett was thinking of making camp when the brush suddenly thinned considerably, then petered out. Starrett looked around, seeing immediately a distant square of light in the gathering gloom. Even as he spotted the light it vanished as if a giant hand had suddenly concealed it.

Shadde remained motionless. 'That's Ray Tolliver's place over there,' he said. 'He lives alone with his wife. We'd better not walk in on them before first light.'

'OK. You make camp back here while I take a look around,' Starrett said without hesitation.

'If it was Ardle shooting at us then we've got to play it safe. He's a real bad killer. If we trap him he won't put his hands up. He'll go down fighting. And I wouldn't be surprised if Tolliver has thrown in his lot with Ardle. They were thick as thieves before the murders took place.'

'I may be away all night.' Starrett took his Winchester from his saddle scabbard and prepared to fade into the shadows. 'If I can locate our ambusher's horse then I'll watch it until the sun comes up and grab whoever comes out to take care of it in the morning.'

He had pinpointed the direction of the light he had seen and went forward until he picked out the faint outline of a shack just ahead. He moved in closer to the small habitation. A cooling breeze was blowing into his face, which afforded him some relief after the long, hot day. The silence was intense, and dim light was afforded by the stars now shining remotely overhead.

Starrett assumed that it was Ardle

who had shot at them, and wondered why the killer was sticking around this area. He circled the crude habitation, moving slowly and well out of earshot. He heard the whinny of a horse somewhere ahead in the darkness and dropped to the ground. His eyes were well accustomed to the gloom and he eased forward a yard at a time, using his ears as well as his eyes. When he was in a position to see the rear of the shack he heard a horse stamp in a lean-to which showed up indistinctly in the gloom, and stayed well away for fear of disturbing the animal.

He eased in against the side wall of the shack and stood for long minutes listening intently. The little building was silent as a grave, and if he had not seen the light from its window earlier he would have guessed the place was deserted. But he knew better. Someone was inside in the dark, and there could well be innocent folk inside, too. He eased away from the shack, moved out beyond the lean-to, and settled down to maintain a lonely vigil.

The dark hours passed slowly. Starrett remained silent and motionless, his patience boundless, his thoughts busy. He was concerned about Del Baker riding out on his first assignment, and could well remember his own first attempt at law dealing. But five years had passed since those days and he had gained much from his subsequent experiences.

Dawn arrived and Starrett gazed at the silent shack. The sun came up, throwing long beams of brilliance across the wilderness. Starrett did not move a muscle. He lay hidden in the brush only two yards beyond the lean-to, his Winchester ready for action. He could hear the horse in the lean-to, and waited out the last minutes of his vigil.

Smoke wisped out of the stone chimney of the shack but no one seemed to be in a hurry to attend the stock. There were two milk cows in a pasture behind Starrett's position, and one of them started lowing insistently. Then Starrett heard the door of the shack creak open. He cocked his rifle.

Presently a man appeared around the rear corner of the shack, carrying a bucket of water. Starrett could see at a glance that this was not Ardle, and assumed it was Tolliver, who owned the place. The newcomer was tall and thin, middle-aged, dressed in drab work-clothes. Starrett was struck by the man's manner, for he seemed nervous, and kept looking around as if expecting a posse to spring out from behind every brush. He carried the water into the lean-to, and Starrett heard him talking to the horse.

Starrett moved in behind the man, confronting him as he turned to emerge from the makeshift stable. The man dropped the bucket, which clattered on the hard ground.

'What the hell!' he declared. 'You near scared me outa my skin, mister. Who are you and what do you want? I don't have any dough, if you've got robbery on your mind.'

'I'm not a thief,' Starrett responded, noting that the horse was indeed a sorrel. 'Who is in the shack?'

'There's just me and my wife here. I'm Ray Tolliver. We don't see folks around from one week to another.'

'I was shot at less than a mile from here as the sun went down last evening,' Starrett said patiently. 'I didn't see the ambusher, but I got a look at his horse, and it was this sorrel. So who was riding it yesterday? Was it you doing the shooting?'

Tolliver shook his head and exhaled his breath in a long sigh. 'No,' he said. 'Not me. There's a man named Ardle in the shack. He's staying with me for a spell. I don't like him being here but he's a bad man and I'm afraid he'll harm me and my wife if I don't treat him right.'

'I'm looking for Ardle. He's wanted for triple murder, and he stole this sorrel from Jefford, the saloon man in Denville.'

'Who are you, stranger? What do you know about Ardle?'

'I'm Buck Starrett, a Texas Ranger — here to take Ardle.'

'You won't get him without a fight,' Tolliver declared.

'I will with your help. I'll follow you into the shack and you duck out of the way the instant you get inside. I'll take Ardle dead or alive.'

'My wife is in there,' Tolliver protested. 'She might get hurt in any shooting. Let me call Ardle outside.'

'OK. Go ahead.' Starrett agreed without hesitation. 'Tell him you found the sorrel lame. I'll get the drop on him when you both come out of the shack.'

'I don't like it.' Tolliver shook his head. 'He'll kill my wife at the drop of a hat.'

'Not if you do like I say. Now get moving. I'll be right behind you. I'm a hair-triggered man so do it right.'

Tolliver shook his head doubtfully and walked towards the shack. Then he turned quickly and swung the empty bucket at Starrett's gun hand. Starrett's pistol was knocked aside but he was prepared for resistance and swayed his upper body backward from the hips as Tolliver dropped the bucket and followed up his action with clenched fists. A solid right punch grazed Starrett's chin, then Tolliver launched himself forward in a desperate attack. Starrett thrust his pistol back into its holster and lifted his hands, meeting Tolliver head on. He threw a hard right that smacked solidly against Tolliver's chin, and then whipped across a left that caught the man flush against the right temple.

Tolliver fell instantly, like a tree struck by lightning. His head hit the ground and he lay still, gasping for breath. Starrett bent, seized Tolliver by his shirt front, and dragged him to his feet.

'Now you've got that outa your system you can get moving,' he rapped. 'And play this straight or somebody will get hurt before the shooting is over.'

They moved around the shack to the door. Starrett ducked below the window beside the door and drew his gun. It was time for a reckoning. He stayed close behind Tolliver as the man opened the door of the shack and entered. Once across the threshold Tolliver dived flat, and Starrett levelled his gun. He saw a woman standing by a stove and a man sitting at a table. The man was in the act of grasping the butt of his gun, which was lying on the table under his right hand. The next instant all hell broke loose.

2

Del Baker rode unhurriedly as he progressed into the great south-west, filled with elation because he was following in his father's footsteps along the dangerous path of administering law and order. But five days after parting from Buck Starrett his high spirits had evaporated and he was more cautious as he neared the little town of Adobe Flat, situated almost on the east bank of the Rio Grande. He reined in on a crest and studied the sprawl of single-storey adobe buildings that formed the town. His first impression of the community was unfavourable. He had stayed the previous night at the Halloran Big H ranch to the north-east, and his uneasiness had grown as he considered the tough cowpunchers who scraped a living from this merciless country.

They had talked of rustlers and

killers; of a gang of Mexicans in particular that came across the Rio Grande at irregular intervals to rob and kill at their pleasure, seemingly immune to the efforts of the local law to stop their depredations, and a name was spoken in awe when Baker asked questions about Adobe Flat: Red Satterfield, a man who ran the little border town and everything in it. Nothing happened around the Devil's Outpost unless Red Satterfield sanctioned it. He owned the big RS cattle ranch to the north, the general store in town, the bank, and everything else worth having. Life was anything but easy on the border, and untimely death was a common occurrence, but life would have been simpler if Satterfield had not gained control around Adobe Flat.

Baker had been jolted into a more cautious frame of mind by what he learned, and there was trepidation in his mind as he prepared to start his assignment. All he had to do was locate

Toke Bellamy, the Circle B rancher, and learn the true situation in this so-called Devil's Outpost while awaiting the arrival of Buck Starrett to lead the assignment.

His horse laboured a little as it cantered into the dusty main street, and he reined to his left to a large barn with a water trough outside. He slid wearily out of his saddle and stood looking around as the horse drank its fill at the trough. A tall, thin man of indeterminate age — anything between forty and sixty — stuck his bearded face around the open doorway of the barn and regarded him with brown eyes narrowed in a suspicious gaze.

'Howdy?' Baker greeted. 'Is this Adobe Flat?'

'It was when I got up this morning,' the man replied with a straight face. 'You're a stranger. Passing through?'

'I ain't got no ambition to stick around, seeing what you have here, which looks like less than nothing.' Baker smiled. 'Are you sure this burg ain't called Boot Hill?'

'It might look quiet at this time of the afternoon, but it sure livens up come sundown. You look like you might have ridden a far piece. Do you have further to go?'

'Not so far now,' Baker replied. He glanced up at the position of the sun, which was well over into the western half of the sky. 'I reckon I'll put up here till morning. Will you take care of my horse?'

'Sure, if you've got money. I'm Joe Kenton. Bring that horse into a stall before it falls down. It looks like it couldn't hobble to the end of the street without using its knees. I don't know about looking after it. I reckon it would be kinder to put it out of its misery.'

Baker grinned and led the horse inside the barn. He produced a silver coin and flipped it into Kenton's ready hand. Kenton fetched a scoop of crushed oats from a nearby barrel and poured it into a manger in the stall which already contained a forkful of hay. Baker stripped his gear from the animal and placed his saddle on a rail.

'Do you have a decent place in this burg for a man to sleep?' he asked.

'Stay away from Satterfield's Hotel. Martha Kenton runs a guest house, and her cooking is the best in town. Her place is on the right after you pass the general store, big place with window frames painted white. She ain't one to allow cussing in the house, or chawin' tobacco. I send a few decent-looking lodgers her way if they call in here first.'

'Martha Kenton,' Baker mused. 'Same name as you. Is she a relation?'

'She's my wife. I take care of the horses that come to town and she caters for the riders. She fills a need. Watch out you don't tangle with any of Satterfield's men. They're likely to shoot first and ask questions afterwards — and that goes for Rafe Millett, the deputy sheriff. Fall foul of him and you'll find yourself breaking rocks for a couple of months as a guest of the county.'

'How will I know who works for

Satterfield?' Baker enquired.

'That's easy. Every damned man in town except me is on Satterfield's payroll.'

'Is that so? Makes it kind of lonely for you, huh? Unless you're in Satterfield's back pocket too.'

'The hell I am! I've got Satterfield's measure. He won't tangle with me if I keep my nose out of his business. We were partners a long time ago but I didn't like his methods so we split up. He leaves me alone because I'm married to his sister.'

'Thanks for the information. I'll look up Mrs Kenton to see if I pass muster. I could sure do with some good home cooking.'

Baker left the barn carrying his Winchester in the crook of his left arm and walked along the street, looking around with interest. He had not expected such a sleepy-looking community at the centre of the area into which he had been sent to hunt law-breakers. But he had not walked a dozen yards before he realized that the name Satterfield was emblazoned around the street. It was over the batwing doors of the big saloon, painted in large black letters on a board in front of the general store, and was etched in the glass of the front window of the bank.

He passed the door of the law office, which stood open, and saw a big man wearing a deputy sheriff's badge, seated on a chair in the doorway. Baker glanced at the man, who appeared to be asleep with his Stetson tipped forward to shield his eyes from the glare of the sun, and wondered if the local law was in Satterfield's back pocket like everything else in the town. He walked on by, but a harsh voice called out. He glanced over his shoulder to see the deputy straightening in his chair and cuffing back his black Stetson.

'Hold on, stranger. I want to talk to you. What's your name and where have you sprung from?'

'I'm Del Baker, on my way to Circle B.'

'Is that so? What business you got with Toke Bellamy? You ain't got the look of a cow hand.'

'If you didn't have that law star on your shirt I wouldn't take you for a law man,' Baker countered.

'So you're a funny man, huh!' The deputy stood up and his right hand dropped to the butt of his holstered pistol. He was an over-large man, carrying many pounds more than his natural fighting weight. His dull-red shirt was stretched tightly across his bulging gut, his arms were heavy but muscular, and his fleshy face matched his general appearance of a human running to seed. His blue eyes were deep-set, looking as if they were losing the fight to peer through their surrounding network of wrinkles, and his mouth was like a trap: lips tight and uncompromising. His yellow hair was long and unkempt, sticking out from under the wide brim of his Stetson.

Baker remained silent. His right hand was down at his side and he could feel the butt of his holstered pistol pressing against the inside of his wrist.

'Was there something else?' Baker demanded when the deputy remained silent.

'I don't like the look of you, Baker.' Rafe Millett shook his head. 'You better turn right around and get the hell back to where you came from. We don't need a wise guy here.'

'I don't reckon to stick around long,' Baker replied. 'I'll be riding out in the morning. I'm fit to travel, but then I didn't carry my horse here — he carried me, so he's a mite tired.'

'Maybe you're deaf as well as stupid,' Millett rasped. 'I said to turn around right now and get the hell out, which in my book means skedaddle pronto. Head back to where you left your horse and make dust, but fast. If I catch sight of you inside of town limits ten minutes from now I'll toss you in the hoosegow.'

'What kind of law do you run around here?' Baker demanded. 'I'm going about my lawful business without making trouble, so where do you get off, ordering me to make tracks because you don't like the look of me?'

'So you're a range lawyer to boot, huh? You reckon you know the finer points of the law, do you? Well, Baker, we make our own laws around here, and you've just run foul of them. Drop that rifle and get your hands up shoulder high. I reckon you've already busted about six local bylaws, and if you don't keep your mouth shut I'll dream up six more and drag you in front of Mort Rickford for a nice legal sentence of maybe thirty days' hard labour and a big fine. We're mighty strict around here with guys who ride in looking for trouble.'

'I'm not looking for trouble and I'll leave this burg tomorrow morning,' Baker said firmly.

Millett flexed the fingers of his right hand. He drew a deep breath and then exhaled in a long, noisy sigh. Baker remained motionless, aware that he had gone further than he meant to, but he could not abide arrogant law men, and this one looked like he had been ruling the roost around Adobe Flat and had got into the bad habit of throwing his weight around.

'You're trying my patience real hard,' Millett said. 'You act like you wanta be tossed in the jug. Now get them hands up or you'll need Joe Peck to tend to you.

'Who is Joe Peck?'

'He's the local undertaker!' Millett grinned, showing his yellowed buck teeth. 'I put a lot of work his way, and it sure looks like you're gonna be his next customer. You got too much lip for your own good.'

The thud of hoofs along the street distracted Millett at that moment and he glanced around to locate the sound. Baker looked in the same direction and saw two riders approaching at a canter.

'Heck, here's Mr Satterfield,' Millett observed. He turned his gaze back to Baker. 'You better make yourself scarce, and don't get into any trouble. I'll be watching you. Be long gone from town by sunup tomorrow.'

'That order falls in with my plans,' Baker said, and turned away. He went on along the street towards Martha Kenton's boarding house, but glanced back over his shoulder to take a curious look at Red Satterfield. One of the riders was ahead of his companion, and Baker assumed that he was Satterfield; a man of around forty-five, big without running to fat, dressed in a good light-blue store-bought suit and a white Stetson. His face was round, fleshy, and set in harsh lines, as if he was naturally ill-humoured. His dark eyes peered alertly from under beetling brows, and thick sideboards of hair showed at his temples in a rich shade of red colour. The chestnut he was riding stood high in the shoulder, a powerful stallion with rolling eyes and a lot of bad temperament in his system.

The man accompanying Satterfield was dressed in drab range clothes; looked lean and hungry, with all the marks of a gunman about him. He wore a pair of Colts on crossed cartridge belts and his right hand was resting on his thigh close to the holstered butt on that side. His eyes were cold, like snake eyes, and were never still: unblinking and watchful.

Satterfield rode into the sidewalk in front of the law office and reined in. Baker, hearing the booming voice of the big man as he greeted Millett, shook his head at the note of arrogance in its tone. Baker continued with easy strides. He spotted the white-painted windows of a square house standing back a few yards from the street with a white-painted picket fence to mark its boundaries. A woman of about fifty was sitting on a bench seat by the open front door of the house with a work-basket on her knees. She was knitting a grey sock, and Baker paused for a moment at the gate to watch her nimble fingers at work, admiring her dexterity. She was wearing a high-necked red dress, and a gold locket gleamed at her throat. Her homely face was unlined, her brown eyes peaceful.

'Mrs Kenton?' Baker called and the woman looked up at him, smiled and put aside her knitting.

'I'm Martha Kenton,' she replied. 'How can I help you, young man?'

'I'm Del Baker, ma'am. I've just ridden into town and left my horse at the livery barn. Your husband said that if I was house-broke you might put me up for the night.'

She smiled as she got to her feet to reveal that she was tall and slender. 'Come right in,' she invited. 'Joe was joking about the conditions I impose because I have never turned away anyone who needs a bed. Will you be staying just the one night?'

'I don't have the option to remain longer.' Baker explained his meeting with Rafe Millett, and saw a shadow cross Mrs Kenton's face.

'I would advise you to do as Millett says for he is a very bad man to cross,' she said. 'I don't know why Sheriff

Brady tolerates him. Millett seems worse than many of the bad men we have around here.'

'It could be a case of setting a hardcase to catch hardcases,' Baker observed. He glanced over his shoulder when he caught the sound of hoofs at his back, and his blue eyes narrowed at sight of the rider who had entered the town with Satterfield. The gunman was gazing at him like a hungry wolf approaching its prey.

'That's Bat Rankin,' Mrs Kenton observed. 'He's Red Satterfield's top gun. I wonder what he's doing out alone? He's Satterfield's shadow, so I expect Red is in town.'

'He rode in with Satterfield a few moments ago,' Baker volunteered, easing his right hand straight down by his side, suspecting that Rankin was coming for him. He was wishing now that he had not aggravated Millett.

Rankin approached and reined in with the nose of his grey almost touching Baker's shoulder. His dark eyes were unblinking, and did not stray from Baker's face. He held his reins in his left hand, his right hand resting close to the butt of his right-hand pistol. Menace seemed to ooze from him, and surrounded him like a deadly aura.

'Mr Satterfield wants to see you, mister,' Rankin said in a grating tone. 'Get a move on back to the law office.'

'Me?' Baker queried. 'I don't know Satterfield.'

'He wants to know who you are, so rattle your hocks. Around here, when Mr Satterfield opens his mouth, everyone jumps to do what he says.' Rankin reined his horse about and rode off back the way he had come.

Baker frowned as he watched the gunman's departure. He had half-expected trouble from Rankin, and relief seeped through his system. He had been told to keep a low profile, but with men like Millett and Rankin on the opposite side of the fence it was hard to stay clear of trouble.

'Be careful of Red Satterfield.' Mrs

Kenton's pleasant face had changed expression. She looked worried. 'Agree with everything he suggests and pretend to go along with his wishes until you can leave town — take everything he says with a grain of salt — and whatever you do, don't antagonize Rankin. He's a cold-blooded killer.'

'Thanks for the advice. I'll see what Satterfield wants, but I'll be back for that room.' Baker turned to depart but paused and held out his Winchester. 'May I leave this with you, Mrs Kenton? I'd like to have both hands free when I talk to Satterfield.'

Mrs Kenton took the long gun. Baker departed and walked back along the street. Millett was seated on his chair in the doorway of the office. There was no sign of Satterfield, his horse, or Rankin. Baker paused in front of Millett, whose eyes were tightly closed, but flickering.

'Where's Satterfield, Deputy?' Baker said loudly, and tapped Millett's outstretched left boot with his left toe.

Millett made a great show of

awakening. He sat up straight and opened his eyes. His face was sullen, as if Satterfield had bawled him out.

'It's you,' he said harshly. 'What are you doing standing here? Mr Satterfield has gone to the saloon, and said for you to see him there. You better get moving. It ain't the thing around here to keep Mr Satterfield waiting.'

Baker made no reply. He walked on along the street to the batwings of the big saloon. He peered over the swing doors into the gloomy room and saw a bartender wiping down the long bar on the right. The saloon was otherwise deserted. The bartender looked up when Baker pushed through the batwings and walked to the bar, his heels rapping the pine boards.

'Are you Baker?' The bartender was short and slightly built. His white apron was a size too large and swamped him. His neck was scrawny and his large head seemed to be out of proportion to his body. He had lank black hair which was slicked down with grease, and wore a black string tie around his scrawny neck.

'Yeah, I'm Baker. Who are you?'

'Charlie Smith. I'm the chief bartender around here.'

'So where is Satterfield?'

'He's waiting for you in his office.' Smith jerked a thumb to the rear of the long room. 'That door under the stairs.'

Baker reached into a breast pocket and produced a coin. 'Gimme a beer,' he said, slapping the coin on the bar top. 'I'm parched right down to my knees.'

'You better see Mr Satterfield first,' Smith observed. 'Nobody keeps him waiting.'

'Gimme a beer, and while I'm drinking it you can run along to Satterfield, if you're worried about him being kept waiting, and tell him I'll be a few minutes yet.'

Smith shrugged his thin shoulders and produced a tall glass of foaming beer. Baker picked up the glass and drank almost half its contents before setting it back on the bar. He wiped his lips with the back of his left hand, heaved a contented sigh, and looked around critically.

'Nice place you've got here,' he observed. 'It gets real busy later on, huh?'

'It takes three 'tenders to handle all the customers when we're busy.' Smith's tone eased a fraction and lost its tension. 'Are you going to work for Mr Satterfield?'

'No. That ain't on the cards.' Baker drained his glass and set it down. He heard the batwings creak and glanced over his shoulder to see Rankin entering.

'You're sure taking your time,' Rankin observed. 'It's a bad mistake to keep Mr Satterfield waiting. Follow me.'

He strode towards the far end of the big room and Baker followed him closely, almost treading on his heels. Rankin paused at the door of the office under the stairs and tapped gently on the door before opening it and looking into the office.

'Here's that stranger you want to see, Mr Satterfield,' Rankin said, and stepped aside, jerking a thumb at the doorway in silent invitation for Baker to enter.

Baker walked into the office and Rankin followed him closely. Baker felt his pistol being jerked from its holster and glanced over his shoulder to see Rankin grinning.

'Nobody carries a gun around Mr Satterfield,' Rankin said. 'You'll get it back — if you leave.'

Baker turned his attention to Satterfield, who was seated at a big desk by a window overlooking a deserted back lot. Satterfield was leaning forward in his seat, his hands together on the desk, thick fingers interlaced. His dark eyes were cold and watchful.

'Where are you from and what is your business in my town?' Satterfield's voice sounded over-loud in the room, and boomed against Baker's ears.

'I ain't from anywhere in particular and I'm just passing through,' Baker replied, disliking Satterfield's arrogance. 'It ain't any of your business, mister, but if you figure it is because you own this town then I'll tell you that I'm gonna spend the night at Mrs Kenton's place before moving on in the morning.'

'I don't like uninvited strangers in my town.' Satterfield sat up straight, his hands sliding off the desk and remaining out of sight. 'Mrs Kenton's guest rooms are all full right now so you better get your horse and ride on before nightfall.'

'Mrs Kenton has already agreed that I can have a room for the night,' Baker replied mildly, 'so I'll be staying. My horse is plumb tuckered out.'

'So you have business around here?' Satterfield persisted.

'No. Like I said, I'm riding through.'

'He's lying, Mr Satterfield,' Rankin cut in. Willett told me this man has the promise of a job out at Circle B.'

'Is that a fact?' Satterfield's hands reappeared on the desk and clenched into fists. 'I don't have many enemies around here, but Toke Bellamy heads the list.'

'That ain't my business,' Baker retorted.

He half-turned as he spoke, reached out to snatch his pistol from Rankin's hand, securing a grip on Rankin's wrist and bending it backwards to put pressure on the gunman's fingers. Rankin gasped in pain and released his hold on the gun. Baker brought his fist up hard and sledged his knuckles under Rankin's chin in a solid uppercut. He thrust the muzzle of his pistol into Rankin's stomach as the gunman reached for his right-hand pistol.

'Hold it right there or you'll be wearing an extra belly button,' Baker rasped.

He grasped Rankin by the shoulder and turned him around so as to step in behind and use him as a shield against any reaction from Satterfield. But Satterfield had not moved, and sat regarding the by-play with impassive gaze. Baker holstered his pistol, drew Rankin's right-hand pistol and tossed it into a corner of the room. Then he did the same with the second gun. Rankin wiped a dribble of blood from a corner of his mouth.

'It goes against the grain to be treated like a criminal when all I want is to get a bite to eat and find a bed for the night,' Baker said through his teeth. 'Is there anything else you wanta know before I leave, Satterfield?'

'If you're looking for a job around here then I can fix you up,' Satterfield said quietly. 'I thought Rankin was top man, and he was until you showed up. But as I hire only the best you can have Rankin's job. He's through as of now.'

'The hell I am!' Rankin snarled. 'You better think again, Red. I know too much about your business to be kicked out.'

'Hold it,' Baker rasped. 'I don't want any part of this. I'll get out of here and leave you two to sort out your differences. I sure as hell don't want to work for you, Satterfield, so let it go, huh? I'm not looking for trouble, but if you figure on giving me some then turn it loose now and we'll settle it before I hunt up some grub.'

Satterfield shook his head. 'You can leave,' he said. 'I reckon you'd be too good for the job I had in mind, and when you leave town in the morning don't ever come back.'

'Hey, this ain't over by a long rope.' Rankin spoke as if his words were burning his lips. 'I'll be looking you up, mister. Nobody makes a fool outa me and gets away with it.'

'You'll be the fool if you push your luck any further, Rankin,' Satterfield cut in. 'Go on, Baker, get out of here. If we have to kill you later, I'll see that you get a good funeral.'

Baker dropped his hand to the butt of his pistol as he stepped backward to the door. He expected Rankin to react, for the gunman could not accept loss of face, and Rankin came around fast, his left hand extending stiffly to block

Baker's draw. But Baker made no attempt to pull his gun. He lifted his hand from his holster, placed his palm against Rankin's chest, and thrust hard by merely straightening his arm. Rankin went backward several short paces on his heels, trying desperately to maintain his balance until he collided with Satterfield's desk and fell sideways to the floor. He sprang up furiously and lunged forward. Baker drew his pistol smoothly and thrust the muzzle against the gunman's chest.

'Call him off, Satterfield, if you've got any control over him,' Baker said. 'He'll likely need one of your good funerals if he pushes this any further.'

'Rap his skull with your gun,' Satterfield replied. 'Maybe it'll knock some sense into him.'

Baker slammed his pistol against Rankin's skull. The gunman groaned, folded to the floor, and lay inert. Baker stuck his pistol back in his holster and departed silently, leaving Satterfield glaring at his retreating back. He ignored the bartender, shouldered through the bat wings, and collided with Rafe Millett, who was in the act of stepping into the doorway. Millett uttered a shout of surprise and tried to avoid contact but tripped over his feet and fell into the dust. He roared with sudden fury and snatched at the butt of his pistol. Baker lunged forward desperately, kicking for the deputy's gun hand.

Baker's toe missed the deputy's gun. Millett uttered a cry of delight and thrust the muzzle of the pistol against Baker's chest. Baker twisted sideways desperately. The muzzle was averted by his movement, but the gun exploded thunderously and Baker felt the lightning flash of a bullet boring into his left shoulder. He slammed his fist against Millett's jaw. The deputy dropped to his knees, trying to lift his gun for a second shot. Baker stepped backwards a quick pace and kicked at Millett's jaw.

The deputy went over on his back and lay still. Baker kicked aside the deputy's discarded pistol and staggered to the alley beside the saloon. He had to make an effort to retain his senses, and he hurried away from the street like a wounded animal seeking sanctuary, not doubting for a moment that the wolves would be out for him now.

3

Starrett saw Ardle flowing into action when Tolliver threw himself to the floor. The killer clawed up his gun and swung the muzzle in Starrett's direction. Starrett heard the hammer being cocked and squeezed his trigger instantly, aiming for Ardle's right shoulder. His pistol crashed and smoke flew. The bullet struck Ardle even as the killer opened fire, and Starrett dropped to one knee as a .45 slug crackled in his left ear. He saw Ardle drop his gun on the table. Blood was already showing on his right shoulder, but the killer scooped up the weapon with his left hand and thumbed back the hammer. Starrett fired again, his muzzle pointing at the centre of Ardle's chest. The shack reverberated with the thunder of the blasting shots. Ardle dropped his gun and went over backwards with his chair.

Gun echoes seemed to hang in the startled air. The stink of burned powder surrounded Starrett, who arose and peered at the motionless figure of Ardle before turning his attention to Tolliver. He was pushing himself up from the floor with relief showing on his rugged face.

'I told you he wouldn't give in without a fight,' Tolliver said.

Starrett looked at the woman, who was standing motionless by the stove with both hands pressed to her face. He motioned for Tolliver to go to his wife and the man did so. Starrett went round the table, kicked aside Ardle's discarded gun, grasped the dead killer by the collar of his coat and dragged him out of the shack.

He dropped the body in the dust and went back into the shack. Neither Tolliver nor his wife had moved a muscle. Both seemed badly shocked. Mrs Tolliver was looking at Starrett through splayed fingers covering her face. Tolliver stood with a protective arm around his wife's shoulders. Starrett's ears were ringing from the thunder of the gun shots. He yawned to get rid of the discomfort.

'Where's the money Ardle stole from the saloon on the night of the shooting?' Starrett asked without preamble.

Tolliver stiffened and frowned. 'Money — what money?' he demanded hoarsely. 'We ain't seen any dough. Ardle was always moaning about being short of money. He wasn't friendly with us, although it might look like he was. He threatened to kill us if we gave him any trouble.'

'Did he say why he was hanging around here instead of riding on when he got clear of town?'

'He said he was owed money and wouldn't leave until he'd got his hands on it. He was waiting for the fuss over the shooting to die down. He was a hard man who wouldn't give up on anything he planned to do.'

'There was a posse out this way right after the murders in town,' Starrett said. 'How did Ardle avoid it?'

'He kept that sorrel well hidden in a meadow in the brush. It was only here last night because he was out watching the trail from town until late. He got restless over the last few days, and I was hoping he would decide to cut his losses and ride out. I think he would have if you hadn't showed up when you did.'

Starrett heard the sound of approaching hoofs and peered out through the open doorway to see his bay approaching with Ike Shadde in the saddle. He stepped outside and Shadde reined in beside him.

'I heard the shooting,' Shadde said, grinning. He slid out of the saddle and went to stand over Ardle. 'I knew that bozo was still around here. I told the sheriff so but he wouldn't listen. Where's the dough he stole from Jefford?'

'Tolliver reckons Ardle didn't have any money,' Starrett said.

'Then he's lying. Let me talk to him.' Shadde went into the shack.

But no amount of hard questioning

or bullying moved Tolliver from his story that Ardle had arrived penniless.

'It stands to reason,' Tolliver insisted, 'that if Ardle took four thousand dollars from Jefford's safe the night of the murders he wouldn't have stuck around here. He would have ridden clear and lost himself in another state. But he was waiting for the trouble to fade, so he said, and then he was gonna ride back to Denville and pick up what was owing to him.'

'I haven't got time to waste around here,' Starrett said at length. 'I've done what I came to Denville for so I'll head on out. Shadde, take Tolliver to town and toss him in the sheriff's lap. I'll come back when I've handled my chore along the border.'

Shadde nodded. 'I always wanted to ride Jefford's sorrel. Get your buckboard ready for a trip to town, Tolliver.'

Starrett was impatient to depart and when he was satisfied that Shadde could handle the chore of taking Tolliver to town he prepared to ride west. He took care of his bay while waiting to see Tolliver and his wife set out in their wagon with Shadde riding behind on Jefford's sorrel, then he headed north-west to pick up the trail to Adobe Flat.

Clearing his mind of Ardle, Starrett rode at a fast pace, aware that he was only a day or so behind Baker. He was concerned about the younger deputy marshal because Baker was still wet behind the ears and inclined to be impulsive, although age would give him the necessary experience to survive — if he lived long enough.

The monotonous scenery was flat and barren. Miles dropped behind Starrett and yet the scenery remained the same, as if he was making no progress. There was scattered brush, sandy soil, and more of the same for mile after dreary mile. The sun glared down from a brassy sky and heat packed into the low places. Starrett rode on, aware that his horse was tiring, but he needed to cover as many miles as possible in haste because he wanted to be right on Baker's heels when the young Ranger reached the Devil's Outpost.

He camped that night by a stream, ate cold food, and then rolled himself in his blanket and slept until the first grey light of dawn streaked the dark sky. He was ready to ride on as the first ray of sunshine crossed the eastern horizon, and he endured the ordeal of riding for the distant border. The day passed, and then the next. He saw very few habitations in this raw land, and not many cattle. A succession of days passed in the same monotonous grind, and he was relieved when he began to pick out landmarks he had been given by Captain Ketchell which indicated that he was getting close to Toke Bellamy's Circle B ranch.

The sun was almost sitting on the horizon when Starrett topped a low hill and saw the collection of buildings forming a cattle headquarters. In this region, where there was a scarcity of timber, most of the buildings were built of sun-dried adobe. There were two barns, four small buildings grouped around a narrow creek with three pole corrals in the background. Standing apart from them was a larger building with a porch in front and a well in the yard to the right. There was no fence around the yard, but two poles had been erected some fifty yards in front of the porch, to which a plank had been nailed, and on the plank, burned into the wood with a running-iron, was a roughly drawn Circle C.

Starrett nudged his horse and rode into the yard, aware that he was seen long before he got within shooting distance. A man stepped into view in the doorway of the nearest barn, holding a rifle at the ready. He came forward purposefully. Several men were standing around one of the corrals, and Starrett noticed that they turned to face him, some of them drawing pistols and holding them ready for action. They all looked wary; ready to start shooting at the drop of a hat.

The guard paused and levelled his rifle at Starrett, who continued to ride forward until he was well within earshot. Then he reined in and eased himself in the saddle, aware of the other men coming forward with ready guns.

'Is Toke Bellamy to home?' Starrett asked, his hands resting on his saddle horn.

'He sure is,' the guard replied.

'Where will I find him?'

'He's up at the house.' The guard gestured with his rifle. 'Sing out when you hit the porch. There'll be a guard just inside the front doorway, and it won't be healthy to just walk in on him. These days, everyone around here is living on their nerves.'

'Thanks for the advice.' Starrett twitched his reins and rode on toward the house.

He dismounted at a hitching rail and wrapped his reins around it. Before he could sing out to announce his presence a man holding a rifle stuck his head out of the doorway, the muzzle of his long gun covering Starrett.

'You got business with Mr Bellamy?' he demanded.

'I sure have, and I've ridden a long way to see him.'

'Follow me and I'll tell him you're here.'

Starrett entered the house behind the guard and they strode along a corridor to a door on the left, which stood ajar. The guard knocked at the door, then pushed it wide and peered into the room.

'Boss, there's a man out here says he's got business with you. Do you wanta see him?'

'Show him in,' a harsh voice replied. The guard stepped aside, motioning for Starrett to enter the office.

Starrett went in and paused before a littered desk, behind which sat a tall, lean man who looked to be in his middle fifties. He had dark eyes that glinted with determination as he looked Starrett over. His deeply tanned forehead was wrinkled, his hair iron-grey and neatly trimmed.

'I'm Bellamy.' He spoke in a clipped tone, as if he was not used to conversation.

'Buck Starrett. Ben Ketchell sent me in response to that letter you wrote him.'

Bellamy nodded. 'How is Ben these days? It's been thirty years since we rode along the border with the Rangers.'

'He's doing fine, and says to tell you he'll drop by himself one day to check on you. He reckons you can handle anything, so there must be a deal of trouble here for you to write to him for help.'

'Sit down.' Bellamy indicated a chair beside the desk. 'We got trouble such as Ben never saw out this way thirty years ago. Adobe Flat, twenty miles east of here, is run by Red Satterfield, who owns just about everything in town, plus a big ranch to the north. Satterfield is a bad man. I have the feeling he's behind my trouble but I ain't been able to prove it yet. Apart from Satterfield there's a gang of Mexican rustlers that is in the habit of coming across the border to hit our herds, and they are real bad trouble. I have to run a big crew — I lose on average a couple of men a month killed by the rustlers, and it is getting hard to find replacements to handle the fighting that comes with the job.'

Starrett nodded. 'There's always been rustling to and fro across the border in these parts,' he mused. 'You haven't mentioned my sidekick, Del Baker. He was a couple of days ahead of me, and planned to report to you on arrival.'

'I ain't seen anyone through here in the past week,' Bellamy said. 'Maybe he rode into Adobe Flat first.'

Starrett shook his head. 'His orders were to come here and talk to you. I guess I'll have to ride into town and check.'

'I'll send a man along with you to show you the way.'

Starrett shook his head. 'No thanks. I'll ride alone.'

'Then you better watch out for Rafe Millett when you hit town. He's the deputy sheriff there — a real hard man. If Baker rode in and crossed Millett's trail then he would have found bad trouble. Millett is in Satterfield's back pocket, and his main chore is to check out strangers riding into town — a job he's real keen on. If a stranger ain't useful to Satterfield then Millett runs him out of town, or worse.'

'So that's the way things are run around here, huh?' Starrett nodded. 'I planned to operate under cover, but if Baker is in trouble then I'll have to work in the open.'

Starrett took his law badge from a breast pocket and pinned it to his shirt front. He was about to rise and take his leave when a knock sounded at the door and the guard looked into the room.

'Bill Rainey has just ridden in, boss,' he said in a tone containing suppressed excitement. 'He's got a bullet hole in his back, and reckons the Mexicans are running off the herd at Longhorn Creek. He knocked a couple of them out of their saddles but was outnumbered so he started back here for help and took a slug as he high-tailed it.'

Bellamy sprang to his feet. 'Tell the boys to saddle up,' he rapped. 'Throw a saddle on my black for me, Tom. This time we might nail that big guy who's bossing those rustlers.'

'I'd like to ride with you, if you can loan me a fresh horse,' Starrett said.

'Be glad to.' Bellamy replied. 'Tom, put the Ranger's gear on my roan. And tell the boys to get a move on.'

The guard departed swiftly. Bellamy went to a gun rack on the back wall and selected a Winchester from the array of weapons. His face was set in a harsh expression as he led the way out to the porch. Starrett followed the rancher closely. They walked across the dusty yard to the nearest corral, where a flurry of activity was already taking place. Hard-faced cowpunchers were saddling up. Starrett's saddle was being transferred to a powerful roan. Bellamy walked to the nearest bunkhouse and Starrett followed him closely. They found a wounded man stretched out on a bunk with a man attending him.

'Is it bad, Cookie?' Bellamy enquired.

'Bad enough,' the cook replied. 'But Bill can take it. I'm having a job keeping him here. He wants to ride out with you but he's leaking blood badly, so perhaps you can talk some sense into him, boss.'

Bellamy bent over the wounded man, whose bearded face was taut with pain. But his dark eyes glinted with determination. He grinned at Bellamy, pushed aside the cook's hands, and made an effort to get off the bunk.

'I nailed two of them, boss,' he grated through clenched teeth. 'There was close to twenty of them, and that big greaser who rides the white stallion was leading them. They've got near to a hundred steers moving to cross the river.'

'Good work, Bill,' Bellamy approved. 'Now stay where you are. You're no good to me leaking blood. Someone has got to stay here and keep an eye on this place, and you're elected.'

'OK, boss.' Rainey slumped back on the bunk and closed his eyes.

Bellamy patted the man's shoulder and departed swiftly with Starrett following. In a matter of minutes a dozen men were mounted and ready to ride. Bellamy swung into his saddle and waved a hand as he set spurs to his horse. He rode out of the yard at a gallop, with Starrett by his side. Dust flew as the tough crew tagged along behind. They followed a trail through the brush, flogging their horses mercilessly, intent on getting within shooting distance of the rustlers.

When the brush thinned and they rode into a wide clearing Starrett saw the glint of water. Night was almost upon them, and Bellamy reined in on the bank of a creek.

'Frank, you and Jake pick up their

trail. One of you can ride back for us when you find it.'

Two of the riders went on immediately, crashing through the brush. Bellamy looked at Starrett.

'It'll be full dark in a few minutes, but we've got to get the herd back before it crosses the river. If I know that big Mexican who runs the rustlers he'll leave a rearguard at the water's edge to stop any pursuit.'

Starrett nodded. A yell attracted them and he looked around to see one of the two men sent to find the tracks of the herd sitting at the edge of the brush and waving a come-on signal. Bellamy fed steel to his mount and set the pace for the rest of them. They rode hell for leather into the shadows. Starrett felt excitement crawl along his veins at the prospect of action against the rustlers, but a remote part of his mind was filled with concern for the missing Del Baker.

Less than fifteen minutes later they caught up with the man who had gone on ahead to locate the rustled herd; he was sitting his mount in cover. Bellamy rode in beside him, and the man lifted a finger to his lips, cautioning silence. From ahead, Starrett could hear the sound of cattle being moved. The night had closed in around them and Starrett could barely see the figures crowding around him.

'We've got them, boss,' the scout reported. 'If we go straight in they won't have time to reach the river.'

'Come on, then,' Bellamy responded. 'Split up into two groups and we'll attack from both sides. Get the drag riders first and then go for the leaders. The herd will stampede soon as we start shooting, and we'll have to turn them before they run into the river. We'll gather them later. Let's go.'

Starrett angled his mount in beside Bellamy as they set off at a fast pace out of the brush. Hoofs drummed on the hard ground and Starrett was aware that they could not sneak up on the rustlers. The brush thinned and then gave way to rough range, and, despite the gathering darkness, he could see the stolen herd being chivvied along by unknown figures.

A gun crashed before they could get within range of the rustlers. One of those riding drag was watching for pursuit, and triggered a warning shot as soon as he heard pounding hoofs on his back trail. Starrett drew his pistol and cocked it. Almost before he was aware of it, they were level with the rear of the herd. Orange-red gun flashes split the shadows, spurting menacingly as the drag riders opened fire while trying to escape. Starrett heard a slug whine over his head. He caught a glimpse of a rider ahead and his gun flamed. The man threw up his arms and disappeared, falling into oblivion from his horse, which galloped on with the herd.

The herd stampeded, running straight ahead in blind terror, activated by herd instinct. The cowpunchers galloped closer, heading for the leaders of the herd and shooting at every human figure appearing before them. Starrett remained close to Bellamy. The rancher wanted to get at the rustler leader, and Starrett went with him. The night was filled with seeming confusion. Guns thundered and riders fell from their saddles, but such were the conditions it was impossible to control the action.

The rustlers left the herd, shooting indiscriminately at the Circle B outfit, but they had no stomach for a serious fight. Bellamy rode in beside the leaders of the herd and fired his pistol into the ground beside their heads. The maddened animals veered away from the shooting. Bellamy stayed with them, aided by his men. They turned the herd to the left, away from the river, and suddenly the steers were running back the way they had come.

Bellamy reined in and waved for his crew to continue chasing the steers. He swung his horse around and rode back to the river with Starrett accompanying him. They halted when their horses splashed into water, and sat looking around. The rustlers had disappeared into Mexico across the river. The last of the gun echoes were fading away across the dark shallow water of the Rio Grande.

'This is as far as we can go,' Bellamy said, and grim satisfaction sounded in his harsh voice. 'We nailed some of the rustlers and saved the herd. The steers won't stop running until they are back on home pasture, and we'll round them up in the morning. I'll send six men back here to watch out for the rustlers sneaking back later. We've done well, but it looks like being a hard day tomorrow.'

They turned their mounts and rode back to Longhorn Creek, where the outfit were trying to settle the frightened herd.

'Is everybody here?' Bellamy demanded.

There was a count of heads and no one was missing, although three men had flesh wounds. Bellamy gave curt orders and the crew organized itself to obey. Half a dozen tough punchers rode back to the river and settled down to watch for returning rustlers. Three men remained watching the uneasy herd and the rest started back to the ranch. Starrett stayed with Bellamy as they rode into Circle B.

'We've got to do something about those damn rustlers.' Bellamy said as they dismounted by one of the corrals. 'But I'm at my rope's end trying to trap them. It ain't the gang of rustlers as such — we must have killed forty of them over the past few years. But their leader is another matter. If we could put him down I'm sure the rustling would stop. But that thieving galoot has got more lives than a cat.'

'Do you have any idea who he is?' Starrett enquired.

'No. I've even sent men into Mexico to try and track him down, but nobody south of the border will talk. He always rides a big white horse, but both horse and man seem to vanish the minute they cross the river. All I've ever got to go on is the prints of the white horse. I almost nailed him a couple of months ago but he got away. I checked for his prints and found them, and I'll know them again if I ever see them. But that ain't gonna lead me to the bozo himself.'

'I'll take a look around in the morning,' Starrett said. 'You can point out the tracks of that white horse for me and I'll see what I can do. But I'm gonna have to find Del Baker before I start my investigation. I can't leave him running around loose.'

'He could still be on the trail between the ranch and where you last saw him,' Bellamy observed. 'He might turn up here during the night, and that will save you riding into town. You better stay the night with us because Adobe Flat would be asleep by the time you ride in there if you left now. In the meantime I'll give you the lowdown on who is who in town.'

Starrett nodded, and when they had taken care of the horses they crossed to the ranch house. A young woman who was introduced to Starrett as Bellamy's granddaughter, Beth, was waiting anxiously in the big front room. Starrett was impressed by her appearance. She was tall and slender, with attractive features, although her blue eyes revealed the great extent of her concern. Wearing a long blue dress which fitted her willowy figure perfectly, she gave colour and homeliness to her drab surroundings.

'No problems, Beth.' Bellamy explained the events that had taken place. 'A couple of the boys got nicked by slugs, but they ain't serious. This here is Buck Starrett. He was sent by my old sidekick Ben Ketchell. I got a feeling now that we're gonna beat those rustlers. We gave them a licking tonight, and tomorrow we'll get down to some serious business.'

'Joe Kenton turned up driving a buckboard just after you rode out after the rustlers,' Beth said. 'He brought a wounded man from Adobe Flat who had fallen foul of Satterfield's crew — was shot by that so-called deputy, Rafe Millett. The man told Kenton he was due to report here, and Kenton delivered him.'

'Is it Del Baker?' Starrett demanded.

'That's the name Kenton gave me. And the man was carrying a Texas Ranger's badge in his breast pocket.' Beth eyed the law badge on Starrett's chest. 'I've had him put in a room in back. His life is not in danger — Kenton had Doc Bannerman check him over before moving him out of town. He has a bullet hole in his left shoulder and will need careful nursing to bring him back to full health.'

'Take me to him, please,' Starrett said. 'I warned him to come straight here and remain out of circulation until I arrived, but he is an impulsive galoot.'

Beth led him through the house to a room at the rear. Starrett shook his head when he saw Del Baker lying on a bed, either asleep or unconscious. Baker's face was pale, his chest bandaged, and he was breathing heavily.

'Kenton said the doctor would be riding out here in a couple of days to check on him,' Beth said. 'The bullet missed the lung but dusted him both sides, so it will be a long, painful time of recovery.'

'You'll tend him, Beth?' Bellamy said. 'He was on his way here to help us, so do what you can for him.'

'Of course,' the girl replied.

Starrett bent over Baker. 'Del,' he called gently. 'Can you hear me? I want to know what happened in town.'

Baker did not respond. His forehead was beaded with sweat. Beth touched Starrett's arm.

'He has a fever,' she opined. 'I doubt he would be able to talk to you even if he was conscious. Leave him be for now. He'll be much better in a few days.'

Starrett nodded and left the room, followed by Bellamy. This was a complication he did not need. But Baker would not have played a large part in the investigation. He had come along mainly to gain experience, and recovering from a bullet wound was one of the hazards of the tough job he had chosen for a career.

'I'll show you where you can sleep tonight,' Bellamy said. 'We'll make an early start in the morning and see if we can come up with an idea to beat the rustlers. If we can put them out of business that'll leave just Satterfield and his crooked organization to handle. Between them, the rustlers and Satterfield are making life tough for everyone in the county.'

'We'll take care of them,' Starrett promised, stifling a yawn. 'The rustlers first, and then I'll ride into town and do something about that trigger-happy deputy.'

'Don't underestimate him,' Bellamy warned. 'He's a cold-blooded killer put into office by Red Satterfield. He wears a law star, but he's no kind of a law man, not even a bad one. Sheriff Brady, over in Birchwood, the county seat, has been told more than once what kind of a man Millett is, but I think he's afraid to go against Satterfield.'

Starrett smiled. 'We'll get around to it,' he promised.

Bellamy nodded. 'We've made a good start,' he replied optimistically. 'But after this it will get a whole lot harder. I've been making a stand against Satterfield and the rustlers, but now you're here, with the full backing of the law behind you, I reckon we'll be able to win this fight.'

'That's why I'm here,' Starrett replied. 'But right now I could do with some shut-eye, and this could be the last peaceful night we'll know for some time to come.'

4

Starrett enjoyed a peaceful night. Bellamy showed him into a guest room and he fell asleep almost as soon as his head touched the pillow. He awoke as the grey light of the new day filtered in at a small window and arose quickly, impatient to begin his investigation. He dressed and went down to the large kitchen, and paused in surprise when he found Beth Bellamy there, doing her morning chores. She smiled at him and lifted a coffee pot from the stove.

'You look surprised to see me,' she said with a smile. 'But I'm always up at the crack of dawn, and with a wounded man in the house to take care of I shall be kept extra busy.'

Starrett sat down at the table. Beth poured coffee into a cup and placed it before him.

'Thanks,' he acknowledged. 'I suspect

that you've been keeping an eye on Del through the night.'

'I looked in on him a couple of times. He's developed a fever so someone has to watch him. But he should be on the mend in a few days, and he looks strong enough to come through this with no complications.'

'If he sticks in the business, this wound will be the first of many he'll pick up,' Starrett observed. 'Law dealing is tough.'

'That is a cynical comment on our primitive way of life,' Beth observed softly. 'How long have you been a Ranger, and how many times have you been wounded?'

'I first pinned on a Ranger badge just over five years ago, and I've suffered three bullet wounds — one fairly serious. But it isn't so bad if you stick to the rules.'

The kitchen door was pushed open and Toke Bellamy appeared, dressed and ready to begin his day. Beth arose to pour coffee for him, then began to prepare breakfast. Bellamy sat down at the table opposite Starrett. The rancher looked tired but seemed impatient for the day to start and was gripped by suppressed excitement. His eyes were fairly glowing with determination.

'Tom Pearce rode in from the river about an hour ago to report nothing doing across the border,' Bellamy said. 'But if those rustlers are going to pay us another visit then they'll show up when the sun starts above the horizon. I'm taking the whole crew out in ten minutes so we'll be in position if there is any trouble. Do you want to come along?'

'I wouldn't miss it for anything,' Starrett responded.

'I looked in on Baker about thirty minutes ago,' Bellamy continued, 'and he seemed to be resting easy. I heard you go to him a couple of times, Beth. How did he come through the night?'

'Once he gets over his fever he should be OK,' the girl said.

They ate the breakfast Beth prepared, and were drinking coffee when footsteps sounded in the front of the house. Bellamy got to his feet and went to the kitchen door. Starrett listened intently as one of the crew made a report.

'Slim Taylor just rode in, boss. There's movement across the river. Looks like the rustlers are coming again. The crew are saddling up. We'll be ready to ride when you are.'

'Be right with you, Joe,' Bellamy replied.

Starrett followed the rancher when he went to arm himself and they left the house as the sun came peeping over the horizon. There was great activity around the corral, but the crew knew what was expected of them, and they were ready to ride within moments. Starrett threw his gear on Bellamy's roan, checked his weapons, and swung into the saddle. They rode across the yard and galloped towards the river.

The herd that had been stolen the night before was grazing in the clearing to which it had returned after the rustlers were chased off, guarded by two alert-eyed cowpunchers. Bellamy rode on, skirting the herd, and headed for the river with his outfit following closely. They were almost within sight of the border when gunfire shattered the silence and ominous echoes fled across the range. Bellamy drew his pistol, spurred his horse, and rode hell for leather through the roseate dawn to get into the action, followed by a dozen resolute cowboys with drawn guns who were grimly determined to beat the rustlers.

The men Bellamy had left to guard the river crossing were down in cover overlooking the water. Gun smoke drifted as they engaged a party of some twenty Mexicans splashing across the river. Starrett immediately saw the big white horse that had been described to him, and reined in to take in details of the Mexican riding it as Bellamy and the rest of his men vacated their saddles and dropped into cover to start shooting.

The leader of the rustlers was a big man with a dark, bearded face who led his thieving crew fearlessly. A wide-brimmed sombrero shaded his eyes and a thick black moustache adorned his upper lip. He was dressed in drab clothing, and had two bandoleers crossed over his chest. He was holding his reins in his left hand and firing his pistol at the cowboys as his big horse came splashing boldly through the shallows of the river. Gun smoke drifted quickly on the morning breeze, but the rustlers came on despite the accurate shooting of the cowpunchers.

Starrett drew his pistol, his gaze intent on the rustler leader. The Mexican pointed his pistol at Starrett, who was the only man standing. The weapon flamed and Starrett heard a slug crackle past his right ear. He dropped to one knee and raised his pistol, drawing a bead on the big man. When he squeezed his trigger the rustler boss jerked in his saddle, fell sideways, and disappeared into the water. The white horse kept running for the riverbank, lunging forward with powerful thrusts of its hind legs. One of the cowboys ran out to grab the animal's reins and lead it out of danger. Gun fire thundered and echoed sullenly.

Starrett looked for the rustler leader but saw nothing in the swirling, fast-moving water. The other rustlers were turning away to flee back across the river, and the cowboys poured a hot fire into them until they were out of range. Rustlers fell into the water and their horses escaped along the river, making for the bank on the Texas side, but more than half the rustlers had been shot out of their saddles by the time the gang reached the Mexican bank. Then the shooting ceased and the cowboys arose from their cover. They stood at the edge of the river, calling out to the rustlers to try their luck again. Starrett reloaded his gun when he saw the Mexicans had no intention of accepting the grim invitation.

'Good work, boys,' Bellamy said. 'We sure gave them a bloody nose this morning. I doubt they'll cross the river again for a long time to come.' He turned to Starrett. 'I was drawing a bead on their boss when you shot him out of his saddle. He went under the water and didn't show again. With any luck that'll be the last we'll see of him.'

'Send a couple of men downriver to check that he hasn't crawled ashore somewhere,' Starrett suggested. 'And look for signs in case any of the rustlers did emerge from the water.'

'OK.' Bellamy told off two men, who fetched their horses and rode south along the water's edge. 'The rest of you take a look along the bank and drag in any bodies that haven't been carried away by the current. We'll give them a decent burial.'

The cowpunchers mounted and rode along the bank. Several inert Mexicans were dragged out of the shallows, and two wounded rustlers were found hiding at the water's edge.

'Take them over to those cotton-woods and string them up,' Bellamy ordered. 'We'll leave them hanging as a warning to any of their pards who figure to come and steal my cows.'

'No,' Starrett said sharply. 'I'll take them into town and throw them in jail. They can stand trial for rustling, but you'll have to prove that they came across the river with the intention of robbing you.'

'Heck, we caught them last night pushing a hundred of my steers to the border,' Bellamy responded. 'That's why I wanta hang them without involving the law. But I guess I can let you do your job properly.' He called to his men. 'Take the wounded rustlers to the ranch and patch them up. The rest of you round up any loose horses and corral them. Let's get cleaned up around here. Tully, you and Johnson remain and watch for any attempt by the rustlers to cross the river again. You'll be relieved in a couple of hours.'

Bellamy left his men to the chore of

clearing up and headed back to the ranch. Starrett rode with the rancher. Bellamy was in high spirits as they dismounted in the yard. The rancher looked around his spread with a smile of satisfaction on his rugged face.

'At last we're making progress,' he said. 'They've been stealing me blind for years and that big guy leading them sure was something else when he came raiding. But it was on the cards that one day he would make a mistake.'

Starrett did not reply. He was looking across the yard toward the house. He stiffened when he spotted a motionless figure lying on the porch.

'Is that one of your men down over there?' he demanded. Bellamy swung around, uttered a curse, and started running towards the house.

Starrett went with him. As they drew nearer to the porch Bellamy rapped in a shocked voice.

'Say, that's Cookie. I left him and the men who were wounded last night watching the place until the outfit came back. What the hell has happened?'

The cook was lying on his face on the porch with a pistol discarded by his side. A trickle of blood had run from his inert body to stain the dusty boards upon which he was lying. Bellamy drew his pistol and cocked it as he ran into the house, calling for Beth. Starrett dropped to one knee beside the cook and ascertained that he was dead. He arose and ran into the house, fearful of what he would discover.

He found Bellamy standing over the prostrate figure of Beth, who was lying on the floor by the door leading into the kitchen. There was blood showing on the girl's blouse. Bellamy dropped to his knees, his rough hands examining the girl, who was breathing; her face pale in shock.

'She's been shot!' Bellamy gasped. 'You better check on Baker. See if he's OK.'

Starrett nodded and hurried from the room. He drew his Colt as he ran through the lower rooms, his feet pounding on the boards. When he entered the room where Baker was lying he found his sidekick unconscious in the grip of fever but not further harmed.

'Del, can you hear me?' Starrett demanded urgently.

Baker's eyelids flickered but he did not come to his senses. Starrett turned and ran back to the big front room, and found Bellamy examining Beth.

'Baker is unconscious. How is Beth?' Starrett demanded.

'She's been shot in the left hip,' Bellamy rasped. 'It isn't too serious. I'll patch her up, but we'll need Doc Bannerman from Adobe Flat.'

'I'll ride in and fetch him.' Starrett turned to the door.

'Just follow the main trail to the east and it'll take you right into town. Doc has got an office opposite the bank. Watch your step. Satterfield is tough on strangers. I told you about his deputy in town, Rafe Millett — a bad man!'

'I'll wear my law badge,' Starrett

replied grimly as he departed.

The roan was standing by the corral with trailing reins. Starrett swung into the saddle, looked around to get his bearings, and then rode east. He picked up the trail outside the yard and pushed the roan into a gallop. Two hours later he was looking down at the main street of Adobe Flat, and urged the roan forward. The street was busy. Starrett looked around keenly as he rode in. He spotted the bank, then saw the doctor's office, with a brass nameplate fixed to the wall beside the door.

Starrett dismounted and entered the office. A tall, lean man of around forty years, wearing a white coat, was bending over a man lying on an examination couch. The patient was bruised and bleeding, and the doctor was talking in a soothing tone while treating the man's injuries. Starrett paused and waited. The doctor looked around at him and then straightened. His blue eyes were calm, his lean features serene, as if his way of life had insulated him against the shocks and alarms of living in the West. But his eyes flickered when he saw the law badge on Starrett's chest.

'Good morning, Ranger,' he greeted. 'I'm John Bannerman, MD. How can I help you?'

'I've come in from Circle B. Beth Bellamy was shot this morning. Her life is not in danger, but Toke Bellamy needs a medical opinion of her condition.'

'I'll ride out to Circle B immediately.' Bannerman was shaken out of his casual manner. 'What happened out there?'

'The ranch was hit last night by rustlers from across the border.' Starrett explained the incidents that had occurred. 'I don't know who shot Beth but Bellamy might be able to tell you all about it when you get there.'

Bannerman nodded. He helped the patient up from the couch.

'The only advice I can give you is to do as that deputy ordered and pull out of town before you meet with more trouble,' he told the man. 'It's a sad fact of life that strangers are not welcomed in Adobe Flat, and Boot Hill has a number of men buried there who ignored Millett's order to leave town.'

'There's a man out at Circle B who rode into town two days ago and was shot by the deputy here,' Starrett said. 'Run your eye over him when you get to the ranch, Doc.'

'I heard about that shooting, but the man had disappeared when I looked for him,' Bannerman said. 'So he made it as far as Circle B.' He nodded. 'OK. I'll check on him. Can you do something about Millett? He's a real menace. He should be put out of business. I tried to get Sheriff Brady, over in Birchwood, to get rid of him but I fear he's too scared of Satterfield to stand up against him.'

Starrett looked at the battered man, who was unsteady on his feet and looked as if he had been pistol-whipped. There were several bruises on his forehead and deep lacerations on his cheeks.

'What's your name?' Starrett demanded.

'Ed Loman.'

'So what happened to you? Were you causing trouble in town when the deputy attacked you?'

'The hell I was. That deputy dropped on to me in the general store. He asked me my business, and then laid into me with his pistol. I never said a word out of place, and the next thing I knew the doc was bending over me. Millett gave me orders to quit town soon as I was able, and I sure as hell ain't gonna stick around here.'

'Hang around long enough to give me a statement of the incident in writing and I'll rope in Millett before he assaults anyone else,' Starrett said. 'Will you do that?'

'OK!' Loman said reluctantly. 'I guess that's the least I can do.'

'If you take my advice you'll have a posse backing you when you start in to tame this town.' Doc Bannerman looked up from checking the contents of his medical bag. 'Satterfield has a stranglehold on this community. He runs all the business that goes on, including the bank, and the men who manage his various enterprises are no better than hoodlums, picked for their prowess with a gun as much as for their business acumen. That bullying deputy can call on any one of half a dozen hardcases who are ready to commit murder if necessary to maintain Satterfield's control.'

'It sounds like an undercover chore,' Starrett mused, removing his law badge and dropping it into a breast pocket. 'If I do it properly then it will all be over before anyone is wise to what is happening. Stay out of sight, Loman, until I come for you. I'll test Millett and see just how good, or bad, he is.'

'Tell me your name before you leave,' Bannerman said. 'We'll need to know what to put on your tombstone.'

'Buck Starrett.'

'Good luck, Starrett.' Doc Bannerman shook his head doubtfully. 'You'll need it.'

Starrett smiled grimly as he departed. He paused on the street and looked around, spotted the law office across the way and took up his reins. He stepped up into his saddle and rode back along the street to the livery barn. Joe Kenton poked his head out of the big doorway of the barn as Starrett dismounted.

'Heck, there's been nothing but strangers riding into this burg in the last few days,' Kenton observed. 'If you can take good advice, mister, you'll get back in your saddle and keep riding. Adobe Flat is hell on strangers right now.'

'You're Joe Kenton, huh?' Starrett countered. 'You took Del Baker out to Circle B.'

'And you're riding Toke Bellamy's favourite roan.' Kenton nodded. 'Things are beginning to add up. If you didn't steal that horse then Bellamy loaned it to you, which makes you an enemy of Red Satterfield.'

'Which would put me on the same side as you, I'm thinking,' Starrett said, nodding. 'How come Satterfield allows you to stand up against him?'

'I'm married to his sister, but he wouldn't like it if he found I was taking an active part against him. How is Baker now?'

'He'll be on his feet again in a week. Would you do something for me?'

Kenton grinned. 'Sure — anything short of killing Satterfield.'

'I'm after Rafe Millett right now. He doesn't know it yet but he's assaulted his last stranger around here.'

'This sounds better by the minute.' Kenton nodded. 'You want me to tell Millett there's another stranger in town, huh? OK, I'll do it. I sure want to see this unfold.'

'I'll be in the saloon,' Starrett said. 'Send Millett along there after me and I'll put a stop to his bad habits.'

'I don't have to warn you that he's a tough cuss, do I?'

'I know his sort. He's got to be taken out.'

'I agree with that.' Kenton grinned. 'Are you working for Bellamy?'

'Let's just say that at the moment I'm

looking after his interests.'

'Sure! But I just hope you know what you're doing. Millett plays for keeps.'

'That's the kind of game I relish,' Starrett responded. 'I'll be in the saloon.'

Kenton nodded and went off along the street. Starrett led the roan to the hitch rail in front of the saloon, wrapped its reins around the pole, and shouldered his way through the batwings. He found the saloon deserted, except for a bartender looking as if he had stopped growing as a youngster. He stepped to the bar.

'Howdy?' he greeted. 'Give me a beer.'

Charlie Smith produced a foaming schooner of beer and Starrett slapped a silver dollar on the bar top.

'Business is looking up,' Smith observed. 'You're the third stranger in three days.'

Starrett picked up his glass with his left hand and drank thirstily. His narrowed gaze flickered around the big room while his ears strained for the sound of boots approaching outside the batwings. When he heard a sound at the top of the stairs on the left his gaze probed in that direction and he saw a man peering down at him. He set down his glass and wiped his lips on his sleeve.

'Looks like you've got a quiet town here,' he remarked.

'It gets a lot busier in the evening,' Smith replied.

'I don't expect to be around that long.' Starrett drained his glass. 'Where can I get some grub in town?'

'There's a diner along the street just the other side of the law office, and a dining room at the hotel that'll serve you any time of the day.'

'Thanks.' Starrett noted that the man at the top of the stairs was unmoving, and his experience warned him not to confront Millett with an unknown man at his back. He moved to the batwings and went out to stand against the front wall of the saloon. He glanced around. Joe Kenton was on his way back from the law office, and a big man wearing a law star on his shirt front was ahead of the liveryman, coming forward like a wild bull trapped in a stockyard, his fleshy face portraying intention and determination.

Starrett went to his horse and put the animal between himself and the deputy. Millett came up and stepped around the roan. Starrett made as if to swing into the roan's saddle although he had no intention of mounting. Millett stuck out his left hand and grasped the roan's reins.

'Hold it, stranger. I want to talk to you,' Millett grated.

'What's on your mind?' Starrett enquired.

'What are you doing with Toke Bellamy's roan? Where are you from and where are you heading?' Millett's right hand was down at his side. His eyes were filled with a feral eagerness.

'What makes you think this is not my roan?' Starrett asked.

'If it is yours then show me a bill of

sale.' Millett's right hand moved furtively towards the flared butt of his holstered pistol. 'I'm guessing you ain't got one, mister, so you better come along to the office with me.'

Without warning Millett swung his left fist in a tight, vicious arc, and his heavy knuckles sped towards Starrett's chin. But Starrett was expecting an attack and swayed back slightly from the waist, just far enough for the fist to miss his chin. He countered swiftly, slamming his right fist into Millett's stomach. The surprised deputy took the full force of the blow with an agonized whoosh of expelled breath. His shoulders came forward as the blow took effect, and Starrett's left fist swung round in a tight little arc that carried all the weight of his powerful body behind it.

Millett jerked backwards, his arms flying wide, his face showing shock and surprise. He hit the ground on his back and lay motionless, his mouth agape, his breathing ragged. Starrett bent over the deputy and snaked the pistol from Millett's holster. He stuck it in the waistband of his pants, then stepped back to inspect his prisoner. Millett's eyes flickered, then opened. He looked up at Starrett's menacing figure. For a moment his gaze was blank, then realization returned to him and his right hand flashed to his empty holster. He scrabbled for a moment in a desperate panic to locate to the butt of his gun. Then he came to the conclusion that the weapon had been taken from him.

'Say, what in hell do you figure you're doing, stranger?' Millett demanded, pushing himself into a sitting position. 'You're piling up bad trouble for yourself. What for did you hit me without warning? I was only talking to you.'

'I hit you before you hit me,' Starrett replied. 'You swung at me for no reason, and I heard that's the way you handle the law around here. So you're the one in bad trouble, Millett, and I'm gonna toss you in one of your own cells and leave you to stew, probably until hell freezes over.'

'You can't do that!' Millett got unsteadily to his feet. 'I'm the damn deputy sheriff around here and nobody is gonna lock me in a cell.'

'You've got a choice,' Starrett said quietly. 'It's a cell or Boot Hill! I leave the choice to you.'

The grim ultimatum silenced Millett and he gazed at Starrett in sudden fear.

'Who are you, mister, and where did you come from?' he demanded.

'I was at Circle B this morning when someone shot Beth Bellamy so I came into town for the doctor,' Starrett said. 'My horse was played out and Bellamy loaned me the roan. So that clears up your doubts about the horse I'm riding, and you can check with the doc. I stopped off at his place and told him what happened out at Circle B.'

'Is that a fact?' Millett drew a deep shuddering breath. He was unsteady on his feet and his face was pale. 'So what's your business in town now? Do you figure to stick around? You don't look like a cowhand to me, so what were you doing out at Circle B? Is Bellamy taking on more gunnies?'

'I wouldn't know about that. I'm riding out after I've had some grub. You got any objections?'

Millett shook his head reluctantly. 'You better forget about locking me in my jail, get your grub, and then pull out fast. There's trouble around here and it's too easy for a stranger to get dragged into it. So what happened out at Circle B? Who shot Bellamy's granddaughter?'

'You'll have to ask Bellamy that yourself.' Starrett heard the batwing doors of the saloon creak open and saw a lean, two-gun man emerging from the gloom — the man who had peered down from the top of the stairs.

'You got trouble, Millett?' the man demanded.

'He was in trouble when he tried to get the better of me,' Starrett said. 'But he's got better sense now, and he's not gonna stir up the water while I'm in town.'

'What happens around here is Satterfield's business, stranger, and he wants to see you now,' Rankin replied. He noted that Millett's holster was empty and eased his right hand closer to the gun butt in his right holster.

'Who is Satterfield?' Starrett demanded. 'I ain't seeing anyone until I've had a meal.'

'He owns this town,' Rankin replied, 'and you better get back in the saloon to see him.'

Starrett grinned. 'He'll have to wait his turn. I'm gonna eat before I do anything else.'

Rankin drew his right-hand pistol with a deft movement. Starrett grasped Millett by the shoulders and pushed him into the gunman. Millett yelled as he fell off balance and collided with Rankin, who tried to sidestep him while attempting to line his pistol up on Starrett.

Starrett jerked his pistol from its

holster and cocked the weapon. Millett spun away from Rankin and fell against the wall of the saloon before dropping to his knees. Rankin stared into the muzzle of Starrett's gun, then dropped his pistol as if it had suddenly become too hot to hold.

'There's no need for gun play,' Starrett said easily. 'Unbuckle your belts and drop the hardware.'

Millett straightened, his fleshy face twisted in anger, but he raised his hands. Rankin stood motionless; hands held clear of his lean waist. His dark eyes were narrowed, watchful with deadly intent.

'I said to get rid of your hardware,' Starrett said harshly.

Rankin moved first. He unbuckled his crossed gunbelts and dropped them into the dust, then stepped back from them, his gaze unblinking on Starrett's face. Millett looked as if he wanted to argue. He had a mulish expression on his face and shook his head, clearly unable to believe the way events had

109

turned against him.

'Don't even think about resisting me,' Starrett warned.

Millett shrugged resignedly and got rid of his gunbelt. At that moment Starrett heard the sound of hoofs along the street and half-turned to take stock of the newcomers. His eyes narrowed when he saw two Mexicans riding in, and his pulses began to race when he recognized one of them as the rustler leader who had been shot out of his saddle at the river earlier that morning. The man was big and bearded, and there was a bloodstain on his right shoulder. Starrett knew that the last time he had seen this man the Mexican had been riding the big white stallion across the Rio Grande.

Starrett felt as if he were in a cleft stick. He was standing in the open with his gun covering two tough men and being approached by a rustler who had been giving the ranchers in the area a real bad time. He had to do something quickly, for the two Mexicans were already beginning to get restive. The rustler boss pulled his horse to a halt and sat with his hand on the butt of his holstered pistol, his face portraying suspicion. The signs were that he would start shooting at the drop of a hat.

Aware that he had to act, Starrett spoke harshly to Millett, who was grinning now, his rapt gaze on the two Mexicans.

'Millett, that big Mexican is the rustler boss who was stealing Bellamy's cows last night — him and about twenty Mexicans. You're the local lawman, so do something about him.'

'Not without a gun in my mitt,' Millett rasped. 'You're making the play, mister, so it's up to you. It looks like you've stuck your hand into a bee's nest for honey and are gonna get yourself stung. You're calling the shots, not me!'

5

Starrett moved to his left, his gun covering the two Mexicans. He heard Millett laugh harshly. Rankin remained motionless, apparently content to watch and wait.

'Millett, that big Mexican with the blood on him was stealing Bellamy's cattle yesterday, so pick up your gun and arrest him,' Starrett said sharply.

'No dice!' Millett snarled. 'It's your game, stranger. I ain't taking your word for what happened out of town, and I ain't about to start a war with Mexicans.'

Joe Kenton's voice rang out across the street and Starrett glanced in the liveryman's direction to see him standing with his back to a wall almost opposite the Mexicans, holding a pistol in his right hand.

'Hey, you Mexicans,' Kenton called.

'Don't stick your noses into this business. Turn around and get the hell out of town.'

'I got all the trouble I need,' the wounded Mexican replied. 'I have come to see the doctor.'

'He ain't around,' Kenton said. 'He's got trouble out at Circle B. I saw him ride out a few minutes ago.'

Starrett could feel sweat running down his face as he waited. The big Mexican grimaced and removed his right hand from the butt of his holstered gun. He shook his reins and turned his horse to start riding back the way he had come, accompanied by his companion. Millett turned his flushed face to Starrett and grinned evilly.

'You got the luck of the devil,' he observed. 'But Kenton will be in trouble with Satterfield for sticking his nose in where it ain't wanted. You'll tell Satterfield about this, huh, Rankin?'

'You can bet on it,' Rankin replied. 'The boss ain't gonna like hearing that a stranger got the better of you, Millett.

You ain't doing your job properly. There's something bad going on around here and you ain't on top of it. Three strangers have ridden in over the last three days and you ain't planted one of them on Boot Hill.'

Starrett watched the Mexicans depart. He wanted to arrest them but had no opportunity at the moment. He turned his attention to Millett and swung his pistol, crashing the barrel across the deputy's head with a slashing movement. Millett collapsed with a groan, and Starrett cocked his gun as Rankin clenched his hands and swayed forward to attack. The muzzle of Starrett's pistol prodded the gunman in the chest. Rankin froze.

'You're acting like you can't wait to get to Boot Hill,' Starrett warned. 'Get Millett on his feet and head for the law office. I'm gonna lock the pair of you in a cell and throw away the key.'

Rankin gazed bleakly into Starrett's determined features and his protest died in his throat. He bent over the groaning Millett, dragged the deputy to his feet, and staggered along the street with Starrett following, leading his horse. Kenton shook his head, said nothing, and tagged along behind. Starrett checked on the two Mexicans. They were cantering out of town. A pang of impatience tugged in Starrett's mind but he smothered it and continued.

It took him only a few moments to bundle Rankin and Millett into a cell in the jail and lock them in. Kenton remained in the outer office, a fixed grin on his rugged features.

'I don't know what your business is, but I like your style,' Kenton said when Starrett joined him in the office. 'But hell will be popping when Satterfield hears about Rankin being jailed.'

'Are you gonna tell him?' Starrett demanded.

'The hell I am! I'm gonna sit back and watch this play. It's time someone put a crimp in Satterfield's set-up, but you'd better be ready for big trouble when he gets wind of this.'

'He'll know soon enough,' Starrett replied. 'I want to get after those two Mexicans. They were in a big war out at Circle B last night and this morning.'

'That big Mexican is Luis Ramirez,' Kenton said. 'He ramrods a hacienda just south of the border, and runs a cattle business — rustles cattle on the side. He's often in town to deal with Satterfield, and judging by what you said on the street just now, it looks like you've pinpointed the man behind Bellamy's troubles. I have done horse deals with Ramirez, but I stay clear of him if I can.'

'Thanks for your help. You haven't done yourself any favours by horning in on my side.'

'It's about time someone pulled on Satterfield's rope,' Kenton retorted. 'He's been running wild for too long. But I don't give much to your chances of putting a kink in Ramirez's tail. He's got an army of greasers who'll shoot anyone just for the hell of it. If you're a lawman come to sort out the trouble we've got around here then you better go back to where you came from and pick up an army to back you.'

'There should be enough men around here with good enough reasons to fight the bad men,' Starrett observed. 'All they need is to be directed.'

Kenton shook his head. 'Satterfield has got this county tied down good and proper.'

Starrett went out to the roan. He glanced around the street as he rode out in the direction taken by Ramirez, and was aware that several tough-looking men were standing around, watching him intently.

'Some of Satterfield's managers and the like,' Kenton observed, as Starrett swung into the roan's saddle. 'They're all ready to shoot on Satterfield's say-so.'

'I'll look forward to meeting up with them later,' Starrett responded, and rode out of town.

Ramirez was heading west towards the border, judging by the fresh tracks

Starrett found on the faint trail. He spurred the roan and set out to ride down the two Mexicans, needing to catch them before they reached the river. He peered ahead but failed to spot his quarry, and pushed on, determined to make an inroad into the investigation facing him. It was obvious to him that Red Satterfield's iron grip on Adobe Flat was responsible for most of the trouble, but the Mexican rustlers were an unwelcome addition to the set-up. Starrett was aware that his troubles would be halved if he could take Ramirez out of the pot.

The tracks led towards Circle B, and Starrett loosened his pistol in its holster as he urged the roan into its best speed. But Ramirez was making surprisingly fast time, and Starrett did not set eyes on the Mexican as the miles slipped by. He saw wisps of dust dancing in the bright air, disturbed by the passage of the Mexicans' horses, but the riders themselves remained too far ahead to be seen. When Starrett eventually reached the Rio Grande he saw Ramirez sitting his mount on the Mexican bank of the river, gazing back.

The Mexican waited until he was certain he had been seen by Starrett, then lifted a hand and waved brazenly before riding on. Starrett gazed after the big rustler, his thoughts churning. He suppressed a sigh, aware that there would be other times and opportunities, and turned the roan to ride on to Circle B.

Bellamy's ranch was like a fortress when Starrett rode in. There were armed guards at every corner, watching all approaches. Bellamy was standing on the porch talking with Doc Bannerman. They paused in their conversation and watched Starrett intently as he dismounted before them.

'I didn't think I would see you alive again,' Bannerman observed. 'How did you manage to ride out of town without falling foul of Millett?'

'Millett tried his trick of bracing a stranger once too often,' Starrett replied, and gave an account of his actions in Adobe Flat. He saw animation filter into Bellamy's rugged face and added: 'How is Beth?'

'She'll be OK in a week or so,' Bannerman said. 'It was a flesh wound she picked up.'

'She told me a couple of Mexicans rode into the ranch while we were out at the river,' Bellamy said. 'She described them, and I've got a sneaking feeling one of them was Luis Ramirez, a no-good greaser who should be strung up.'

Starrett nodded and explained how Ramirez had ridden into Adobe Flat. 'He had a bullet hole in his right shoulder, and I recognized him immediately — he was the rustler boss riding the white horse at the river this morning. I had my hands full at that moment with Millett and Rankin. I tried to catch Ramirez after I had jailed them. But he rode across the river, and thumbed his nose at me when I last saw him.'

'So Ramirez is leading those Mexican

rustlers,' Bellamy observed. 'Huh, I must be getting old — I should have put two and two together and worked that out for myself. But he's rustled his last steer on this side of the border! I'll take my crew across the river tonight and hit him where it hurts.'

'I'd rather work from the other end of the trouble,' Starrett said. 'I want to break Satterfield's hold on Adobe Flat and bring law and order back to the town before dealing with the rustling.'

Bellamy grimaced but nodded. 'OK. I'll go along with that. Now we're wise to Ramirez we can hold him at bay until you're ready to stop him. So you're gonna tame Satterfield, huh? I'd sure like to see that, but you won't be able to handle it on your own. Satterfield is as big a threat to Circle B as Ramirez, so we'd better work together. Deputize my crew and we'll act as a posse. We've taken all we're going to from Satterfield, so let's ride into town and face him down.'

'You'll need your crew here on the

ranch to confront Ramirez, if he shows up again,' Starrett mused. 'I'll feel happier working from another direction. I'll get the county sheriff to appoint an honest deputy to take over in Adobe Flat, and then sap Satterfield's power by due process of the law.'

'It'll take a lot longer doing it your way,' Bellamy said grudgingly. 'If you rode back to town with my crew backing you it would all be settled by the time the smoke cleared. But that's the way we used to do it in the old days. You young fellers have different notions now. What I wouldn't give to have a dozen of the old Rangers behind me now!'

Starrett smiled. 'Tell me about them sometime! But in the meantime you could send a man to tell the county sheriff about the situation in Adobe Flat. I'll head back to town and keep the situation under control until I get more help. How is Baker this morning?'

'I've had a look at him,' Doc Bannerman said. 'He'll be up and about in a few days. But he'll be no good to you for a time. Can't you get in touch with Ranger headquarters and fetch more help out here?'

'The Rangers are stretched pretty thin on the ground right now,' Starrett said. 'I shall make a report on the situation, but I know I won't get any extra help. They'll expect me to handle the situation. So I'd better stir myself and head back to town. Thanks for the use of the roan, Bellamy. I'll shift my gear back to my bay now.'

'I wish you would take a couple of my best gunnies with you,' Bellamy said. 'You'll need someone to watch your back. Satterfield will be waiting for you when you return to town. He can't afford to let you run loose.'

'Thanks for the offer. I'll let you know if I do need any help.'

Starrett led the roan across to the corral and shifted his saddle and gear to his own horse. When he was ready to ride he went back to the house, and found Doc Bannerman waiting for him.

'I'm heading back to town now,' Bannerman said, 'and I could do with some company. Maybe I can fill you in on local background while we ride.'

'Sure,' Starrett said. 'I'll take a look at Baker before we make tracks. I could have done with his help right now, but I'll see it through.'

Bellamy accompanied him to Del Baker's room. Starrett found the young Ranger awake and impatient to get into the action. Baker's eyes gleamed when Starrett recounted his experiences in town.

'I hope you'll let me handle Millett when I'm up and about again,' Baker said.

'If he's still in jail when I get back to town then that's where he'll stay for a long time,' Starrett said. 'You concentrate on getting back on your feet, Del. There'll be plenty for you to do when you're fit again.'

Baker grimaced. Starrett took his leave and rode out with Doc Bannerman. They hit the trail to town. Starrett had not progressed more than a mile when he got an uncanny feeling that they were being watched by unseen eyes. He said nothing to the doctor, who was chatting animatedly, but kept his surroundings under close observation, looking for tell-tale dust, sunlight glinting on metal, or any kind of movement in the barren wilderness. The brush was thick in places, and Starrett tingled at the thought of being ambushed.

'Don't look over to your left,' Bannerman said casually. 'There's a small rise, and two riders are sitting their mounts there, watching us. They look like Mexicans. Do you think the rustlers are about to attack Circle B again?'

Starrett checked out the rise without turning his head. He caught a faint sign of movement but did not see the riders.

'I had a feeling we were being watched just before you spoke,' he said. 'We'd better keep going as if we've seen nothing, and when we're clear I'll ride back to see what is going on. If the

Mexicans are about to hit Circle B again you can bet Bellamy won't be caught on the wrong foot.'

They continued, and Starrett watched his surroundings alertly, his fighting instincts aroused. Moments later he picked out the vague outline of a rider sitting his mount on a skyline over to his right, and his teeth clicked together when he saw the man was wearing a sombrero, high-crowned and big-brimmed. The fingers of his right hand moved instinctively to the butt of his holstered pistol but he restrained the movement and kept riding as if he had seen nothing, aware that the Mexicans would shoot him out of his saddle without hesitation if he showed any signs of hostility.

But they rode through the area without trouble. Half a mile further along the trail they rode into dense brush which swallowed them up and concealed their movements. Starrett reined in, drew his pistol, and examined it.

'I'll swing out a mile or so to the left and circle back to the ranch,' he told the uneasy Bannerman. 'You'd better head back to town, Doc. Don't get mixed up in this fight. I'm thinking you'll be needed when the shooting is over.'

'I guess you know what you are doing,' Bannerman replied. 'There'll be at least a score of those rustlers, I reckon, so you'll have to use your head to get the better of them.'

'Thanks for the advice, but I can handle it,' Starrett responded. 'See you around, Doc.'

Bannerman nodded and rode on. Starrett sat his mount in cover, steeling himself for action. He moved out to his left and rode cautiously, staying in cover and working around in a circle to get behind those Mexicans he had seen. He did not think Bellamy could be caught napping, but if the rustlers were present in sufficient numbers they could swamp the tough Circle B cowhands. He began to revise his assessment of Luis Ramirez, and decided to keep an open mind on how to handle this complex trouble facing the county.

He found a brush-choked draw heading in the direction he wished to take and reined his horse into its cover. He had to force his way through dense brush in places, and was concerned that he was making too much noise in his approach. But he reached the top end of the draw without incident and reined in on a bare rise overlooking a barren stretch of broken ground. He dismounted and moved the horse off the skyline.

Five horses were tethered in a cluster of copper-coloured rocks just in front of and below him, and Starrett, looking around for their riders, caught sight of a figure seated in the cover of a tall rock, guarding the animals, while four other men sneaked towards the distant Circle B with rifles in their hands. Starrett looked around intently to check the total number of rustlers, hoping there were just those five whom he could see, but he soon spotted another group of seven figures off to his left, mounted and obviously waiting for those men afoot to get into a position overlooking the ranch.

The guard looked to be half-asleep, leaning back against a rock with his sombrero pulled low over his eyes, but Starrett was startled when the man suddenly pushed back his broad-brimmed hat and lifted a rifle to his shoulder. The crash of a shot hammered and the bullet plucked at the crown of Starrett's Stetson. He ducked hastily as a string of raucous echoes fled across the barren range.

Starrett snatched his Winchester from its saddle boot, jacked a cartridge into the chamber, and snapped a shot at the man as he scurried around the rock into cover. The blade of his foresight was lined up on the Mexican's body as he fired, and his 44.40 slug struck the man in the left hip. The guard went down in a heap, yelling in agony, his legs threshing as he scrambled awkwardly out of sight.

Starrett looked around quickly. The

other men were looking in his direction, and almost immediately slugs began crackling around him. He dropped flat and crawled to the right before easing up to observe. The man he had shot was waiting for him and opened fire with his rifle, clipping bits off the brush surrounding Starrett and raking the entire area.

Heavy echoes hammered away into the distance. Starrett kept low and crawled to his right, wanting to circle the wounded man. He saw the riders push forward over a ridge and head into Circle B, and moments later a ripple of shots blasted out the silence, which was answered by a volley of defensive fire from the ranch. Starrett was relieved by the knowledge that Bellamy and his tough outfit had not been caught napping.

Starrett saw the crown of a sombrero showing above a rock where the wounded guard had gone to ground and put a slug through it, sending it whirling in the air. The man arose some feet away from the position of the hat and drilled the air around Starrett with a stream of accurate shooting. Starrett ducked, moved to his right, and craned up again. He saw the chance of a clear shot and fired instantly, catching the man in the act of ducking, but Starrett sensed that he had scored another hit for the man dropped out of sight and did not fire again. Starrett continued to circle, and moments later he reached a position from which he could see the guard, who was lying unmoving on his face.

The shooting beyond the ridge continued as the attackers moved in. Starrett went back for his horse and led the animal off the rise. He stepped up into his saddle, his rifle cradled in his left arm, and headed for the spot where he had last seen the four dismounted riders. When shots thudded into the brush around him he dismounted in a flying leap and, still holding his Winchester in his left hand, drew his pistol and cocked it.

Two men were coming back towards him, running from cover to cover, shooting rapidly to put Starrett's head down. Starrett dropped to his knees and lifted his pistol. He fired without seeming to aim and one of the pair finished his headlong charge in a flattened dive that took him into cover. The second man paused and took his time to draw a bead on Starrett, who beat him to the draw and fired two quick shots. The slugs smacked into the Mexican and he dropped instantly, blood spurting from two big holes in his chest.

Shots were hammering and echoing across the bleak range. Starrett moved forward again, aware that he was sweating profusely. He angled towards the spot where the remaining two men afoot had vanished from his view, and worked his way up a slope to a low ridge where he could see gun smoke swirling on the stiff breeze. He saw two sombreros in a position on the ridge and stalked them, intent on cutting down the number of attackers shooting at the ranch.

The volume of shooting from the area where the seven riders had vanished rippled like rain beating on a tin roof. Starrett paused to look around and check the men he had shot. He could see them sprawled inertly in the brush, out of the fight and apparently dead. He reloaded the empty chambers of his pistol before moving on.

He came quite suddenly upon the two men hunkered down on the ridge. They were close together and intent on tossing slugs into Circle B. The nearest man caught a faint movement out of a corner of his eye and swung in Starrett's direction, his rifle lifting. Starrett shot him between the eyes and he fell sideways against his companion. Starrett fired again and the second man slumped inertly.

Starrett removed the guns from the men before peering over the ridge at the ranch. He could see loose horses in the brush on the slope that led down to Circle B, and a number of dismounted men were hunkered down in the brush, firing rapidly at the ranch. Gunsmoke was drifting across the ridge, and a heavy volume of fire emanated from the ranch buildings below as Bellamy's outfit resisted the attackers.

There was no chance of the attackers overpowering those men ensconced in cover down on the ranch, Starrett could see at a glance, and he estimated that Bellamy's crew could hold on indefinitely. The attackers were beginning to waver. Four of the seven riders were still in the fight, and two of them were already pulling back, darting from cover to cover to withdraw to the ridge where Starrett was waiting.

The shooting from the ranch intensified. Starrett holstered his pistol and levelled his rifle. He opened fire on the men in the brush and downed two in as many moments. The surviving two started to pull out, and when they came under fire from Starrett they hunted fresh cover and returned fire. Starrett kept up a steady rate of fire, his slugs beating through the brush, and first one and then the other man pitched to the ground. The shooting faded slowly until an uneasy silence settled over the range.

Starrett stood up cautiously, revealing himself to the defenders at the ranch. Toke Bellamy emerged from the ranch house and waved. Starrett returned the salute, then started down the slope to check on the fallen attackers as Bellamy and some of his men came up to meet him.

The nearest attacker lay on his face, arms outstretched and rifle discarded at his side. Starrett turned the man over and removed the big sombrero shading his features. Shock speared through him when he saw that the man was not Mexican but a North American. He went down the slope quickly, intent on checking the rest of the attackers. He stood shaking his head in disbelief when he discovered they were not Mexicans at all.

6

Bellamy was smiling when he reached Starrett. His face was grimed with gunsmoke but he was happy.

'I thought we were in for bad trouble when they started shooting us up,' he said. 'But when you took them from the rear they didn't stand a chance. In view of this attack I think you should concentrate on Ramirez first, don't you? This is the third time he's come at us since last night.'

'Take a look at them,' Starrett said, 'and tell me if they are Ramirez's men.'

Bellamy frowned at the tone of Starrett's voice and turned his attention to the dead man lying in front of Starrett.

'Hey, he ain't Mexican!' he observed. 'Boys, check out those other men and see if there are any Mexicans among them.'

'There are twelve of them altogether,'

Starrett observed, 'and we nailed them all. Some of them will be wounded, so we might get some information from them. What do you make of this, Bellamy? Does Ramirez operate with men from this side of the border?'

'He deals with North Americans, but I doubt if he has any of them riding with his rustlers. So who are these men?'

'For a start, check them out and see if you can recognize any of them,' Starrett advised.

Bellamy nodded and went around the fallen riders. Starrett fetched his horse, and checked the men he had killed on the ridge. One was a Mexican, but the others were not. He rode back to where Bellamy and his crew were gathering in the bodies. Bellamy was shaking his head.

'Most of these men are not Mexican,' he told Starrett.

'There is one Mexican on the ridge,' Starrett countered.

Bellamy told his men to bring in all the bodies, and he and Starrett went down the slope to the ranch. Bellamy heaved a long sigh, but his expression was filled with uncertainty when he glanced at Starrett.

'What do you make of this?' he demanded. 'I thought my rustling problems came through Ramirez and his crew, but now I'm not so sure.'

'Ramirez might be trying to play it smart,' Starrett mused. 'He could have hired a gang of white rustlers to throw you off his tracks. I guess there is one sure way of checking out the situation. I'll follow the tracks this bunch left when they came in and find out where they started from.'

'I was thinking that's the only way.' Bellamy nodded. 'Take a couple of my top men along with you. You might need some help. Joe Lunt is good at tracking, and Pete Spencer is fast with a gun.'

'OK.' Starrett agreed without hesitation. 'I'll ride out now.'

Bellamy looked around, and called to a couple of his crew. 'Joe Lunt and Pete Spencer,' he introduced when the men arrived. Lunt was tall and thin, with an angular face and a prominent chin. His pale-blue eyes were narrowed as he listened to Bellamy's orders. Spencer was short and broad-shouldered, and wore his holstered pistol on his left hip, butt forward. He nodded silently when Bellamy spoke.

'Ready when you are, Starrett,' Spencer said.

'Hey, boss,' one of the other riders called. 'Guess what! One of these guys is Al Toomey.

'The name sounds familiar, Carter,' Bellamy replied. 'So who in hell is he?'

'He hangs around Adobe Flat,' Doug Carter replied. 'He ain't got a regular job. Satterfield employs him when he needs an extra man for anything. Toomey's done just about everything in town in the last six months, except run the bank.'

'Throw him across a saddle and I'll take him into town,' Starrett said instantly.

'That might not be a wise move,' Bellamy warned.

'It could be the break I'm looking for.' Starrett nodded. 'Send Lunt and Spencer out to trail those riders back to where they came from, and they can report to me in town when they have something to talk about. I'll go back to Adobe Flat and start some serious law dealing. Put the rest of these corpses in a wagon and send them into town. We might just find someone who knows what is going on.'

Bellamy nodded and snapped fresh orders to his men. The body of Art Toomey was roped to the saddle of a horse and Starrett held the reins in his left hand when he started out for town. He rode with a grave warning from Bellamy, but he was committed to his job and pushed along the trail to Adobe Flat, followed closely by the horse carrying the remains of Al Toomey.

★ ★ ★

It was late afternoon when Starrett saw the roofs of the town in the distance.

He approached the main street cautiously, and reached the stable without sighting any of the townsfolk. He rode into the big barn and stepped down from his saddle, looking around for Joe Kenton. The stableman was not in the barn, and Starrett wondered what had occurred in Adobe Flat since he rode out earlier. He loosened his pistol in its holster, swung into his saddle and led the rustler's horse out to the street.

Starrett rode along the street, his gaze flickering around the town. Someone peered out over the batwings of the saloon as he passed, uttered an exclamation, and ducked back inside. Starrett continued to the law office and dismounted outside. As he wrapped his reins around the hitch rail the law office door was opened and he looked up to see Rafe Millett emerging. Millett saw the dead man on the horse and halted in mid-stride, his mouth gaping in shock. He turned his head to look at Starrett, recognized him, and reached for his holstered gun in a fast draw.

Ready for action, Starrett drew his Colt smoothly. He cocked the weapon and fired before Millett cleared leather. His slug smashed into Millett's left leg just above the knee. Millett didn't finish his draw. He yelled in agony as he twisted and fell to the ground, the crash of Starrett's shot drowning out his cry.

'Who turned you loose from your cell?' Starrett demanded as the gun echoes fled.

Millett looked up at him, a grimace of agony on his fleshy face. Both his hands were clasped around his lower thigh and blood trickled between his splayed fingers. Starrett stood over Millet, his smoking pistol pointing its black muzzle at the deputy's head.

'I asked you a question,' Starrett said sharply. 'If I don't get an answer in one minute flat then you'll be nursing a bullet in your other leg, so start spouting, and tell me the truth.'

'The blacksmith busted the lock on the cell door,' Millett gasped. 'I am the deputy sheriff of this burg!'

'Not any more,' Starrett said quietly. 'I've taken over. But perhaps I didn't make that clear this morning when I locked you in a cell. You're finished around here, Millett.' He reached down and ripped the law star from Millett's shirt front.

'You can't do that,' Millett protested.

'I've just done it.' Starrett smiled. 'Listen to me, and answer my questions truthfully. The dead man on the horse is Al Toomey, in case you don't recognize him, and he was riding with a bunch of men who shot up Circle B today. What do you know about Toomey? Who does he work for?'

'He never had a regular job,' Millett replied. 'Send someone to fetch the doc. I could bleed to death while you're jawing. I saw Bannerman ride in some time ago.'

'All in good time,' Starrett retorted. 'Answer my questions. Where is Joe Kenton? He's not in the stable. Has anything happened to him because he helped me out this morning? There'll be hell to pay if he's been harmed.'

Millett's expression hardened and he clenched his teeth. He gazed up at Starrett with defiance glinting in his eyes Starrett pressed the muzzle of his pistol against the deputy's right thigh. He cocked the gun and Millett flinched; his face turned pale.

'You know what to expect if you don't talk,' Starrett said. 'And I want the truth. What's happened to Joe Kenton?'

'He's in a cell back there.' Millett jerked his head towards the law office. 'Kenton is Satterfield's brother-in-law, and that's why he ain't dead for helping you this morning. I was told to keep him behind bars until tomorrow.'

'On Satterfield's orders, I guess.' Starrett nodded. 'OK, I'll be talking to Satterfield shortly. Now get up and go into the jail. I'm putting you back in a cell, and this time no one is gonna bust you out. If anyone does try to free you then you tell them you wanta stay behind bars, or I'll put you out of circulation permanent. You got that?'

'Just get the doc over here,' Millett said. 'With this leg I'm going no place for a spell.'

'You'll be in jail for a lot longer than you imagine, if you've been pulling the tricks I suspect,' Starrett told him. 'Now move, and don't even think of trying to get the better of me.'

'Who are you?' Millett demanded as he lurched to his feet. 'You can't come into this town and throw your weight around.'

'So stop me, if you think you can.' Starrett reached into a breast pocket and produced his Ranger badge — a small star set in a silver circle. He put it on his vest, and saw Millett's eyes widen.

'So that's it.' Millett groaned. 'I'll do a deal with you, Ranger. I'll tell you what's been going on around here if you'll turn me loose afterwards.'

'I know what's going on,' Starrett retorted. 'I wouldn't trust you any further than I could throw a full-grown buffalo. You're going back in a cell.'

'If you do know what's going on then you're a fool for riding back here alone,' Millett said through clenched teeth. 'You ain't got a chance.'

'I make my own chances. You know where the cells are so get moving. I'll make you comfortable behind bars before I fetch Doc Bannerman.'

Millett limped into the law office, bent over and clutching his right thigh. Starrett saw a bunch of keys on a desk that was situated to catch the light from an alley window and picked them up. He put a hand on Millett's thick shoulder and pushed the deputy across the office. Millett clutched at Starrett's left arm as he lost his balance, and Starrett fended him off.

'You can't lock me up without a charge.' Millett paused at the door which led into the cells.

'You assaulted a man named Ed Loman. I've talked to him and he's gonna make a statement that will cover it.' Starrett grinned. 'You finally went too far, Millett, and now you'll pay for the way you've been handling the law around here.'

'This is Satterfield's town. He owns it lock, stock and barrel. Do you reckon he's gonna let you come in here and tear down what it has taken him years to build up? My guess is that you're living on borrowed time, Ranger, and it is getting mighty short.'

'Put a rein on your tongue unless you've got anything to tell me about the situation in town. Get moving. The sooner I've got you behind bars the sooner you'll have the doctor in here.'

Millett pushed open the door and walked into the cell block. He entered an empty cell, threw himself on a bunk, and Starrett locked him in. Joe Kenton was standing at the door of an adjoining cell. He shook his head slowly when Starrett went to him.

'Does this mean I'm free?' Kenton demanded.

'It sure does. But how do you stand with Satterfield?'

'I'll take my chances with him,' Kenton

said. 'I need to get back to the stable. But you better watch out for Bat Rankin. He'll be watching for you. Satterfield has told him to take you out.'

'Did you actually hear Satterfield say that?' Starrett demanded.

'Yeah, but I don't reckon I'll stand up in a court and admit it.' Kenton shook his head. 'I have to live here, and although I can get away with some things because Satterfield is my brother-in-law, there is a limit to what he'll take.'

'I'll be talking to Satterfield, and I expect him to pull in his horns when I put him straight.'

Kenton grimaced. 'I don't think talking will do anything. Satterfield has got the bit between his teeth and the only thing that will stop him is a bullet in the head.'

'Let me worry about that,' Starrett said. 'You'd better watch your step after this.'

Kenton led the way into the office. Starrett caught a movement by the street door and peered past Kenton to see Doc Bannerman entering, carrying a brown medical bag.

'I heard a shot,' Bannerman explained. 'Is there anyone I can help?'

'Millett is in a cell with a bullet in his leg.' Starrett turned back to the cells. 'I'll let you in, Doc.'

'I'll be getting back to my stable,' Kenton said. 'Take it easy, Ranger, or there'll be blood on the street.'

'I'll see you later,' Starrett promised. 'Thanks for your help this morning.'

Kenton departed and Starrett accompanied Bannerman into the cells. He unlocked Millett's cell and the doctor entered. Starrett handed the cell keys to Bannerman.

'Lock him in when you've tended him, Doc,' he said, 'and I'll pick up the keys later. I have to move pretty fast now.'

'You're gonna try and clean up the town on your lonesome?' Bannerman asked.

'That's how it's done in the Rangers.' Starrett shrugged. 'See you later, Doc.'

Bannerman shook his head in disbelief. Starrett left the office and paused on the street to look around. A small knot of men were standing in front of the bank, and Bat Rankin was one of them. Starrett dropped his right hand to his side and walked steadily towards the group. The townsmen began to scatter, but Rankin stood his ground, facing Starrett, his gaze steady and his expression bleak.

'I left you in jail when I pulled out of town this morning, Rankin,' Starrett called as he approached the gunman.

'You made a big mistake,' Rankin replied, 'and we'll put that right here and now. So you're a Ranger! I guessed as much, but that badge counts for nothing around here. You made another mistake by coming back to town. Pull your gun and start shooting.'

Rankin reached for his pistol as he spoke. Starrett reacted without conscious thought. His right hand came up gripping his pistol. Rankin was fast, his draw a blur of deadly speed. Starrett's thumb cocked his gun as it cleared the holster, and he fired the instant the weapon was levelled at Rankin. The raucous crash of the shot thundered around the street, followed by Rankin's shot, which sounded like an echo. But Starrett's slug struck Rankin in the chest before the gunman could level his Colt and his bullet thudded harmlessly in the dust. Rankin's hand opened convulsively, spilling his gun, and he followed it down in a threshing heap, his legs kicking spasmodically before he relaxed inertly.

Starrett stood motionless until the gun echoes faded. Then he holstered his gun and went on towards the saloon. Men came out of cover and converged on Rankin's body, talking in hushed tones as they gazed down upon the bloodstained gunman.

The interior of the saloon was gloomy, deserted except for the bartender standing by the stairs which led to an upper storey.

'Where are you going?' Starrett demanded.

'Who in hell are you?' Charlie Smith

demanded. His expression changed noticeably when he saw the Ranger badge on Starrett's shirt front. 'I heard shooting on the street,' he added, 'and I'm gonna tell Mr Satterfield.'

'Where is Satterfield?'

'There, in his office.' The bartender jerked a thumb at the door under the stairs.

'So I'll talk to him. You get behind the bar and stay there.'

The man obeyed without demur. Starrett strode across the long room, his heels thudding on the pine boards. He reached the office door and thrust it open without warning, his right hand down at his side as he entered. The inside of his right wrist was touching the butt of his holstered gun. He paused on the threshold, closed the door with his heel, and angled to the left as he approached the desk across the room. His gaze was intent on the big man seated behind the desk.

'Mr Satterfield, I guess,' Starrett observed. 'You're the big man of Adobe

Flat, so I'm told. I'm Buck Starrett, Texas Ranger, and I've been sent here to bring law and order back to the area.'

'Is that so? Then why come in here? I'm a busy man and there's nothing I can do to help you. What was the shooting I heard?'

'Your man Rankin drew on me.'

'And where is he now?' Satterfield straightened in his seat, his eyes taking on a pale glitter as he guessed at Rankin's fate.

'Gone to hell, I shouldn't wonder,' Starrett said callously. 'You'd better call off your gunnies, Satterfield. I've put Millett back behind bars, and this time he won't be sprung. You're running this town but you'll toe the line now. There'll be no more strong-arm stuff unless I handle it.'

'Are you here alone?' Satterfield demanded.

'I can have twenty tough Rangers here in a matter of days should I need them, but I think I can handle this without too much trouble. The thing for you to remember is that because you own the town you will be held responsible for any future trouble, and if I get any resistance from your men I shall come for you. I'll throw you in a cell and lose the key.'

'The hell you say!' Satterfield started to his feet, his expression hardening. He was wearing a gunbelt, and dropped his right hand to the butt of his holstered pistol.

'Hold it right there!' Starrett warned. 'You'll need to be a lot faster than Rankin to have any chance against me. Get rid of your gun, and use only your index finger and thumb. Then sit down and place your hands palms down on the desk. I haven't finished with you yet.'

Satterfield paused, a muscle working spasmodically in his left cheek. His cold eyes were narrowed and calculating. Then he exhaled in a long sigh and discarded his gun, tossing it into a corner of the office. He sat down in his seat and placed his hands on the desk, his thick fingers splayed.

'So what's on your mind?' he demanded.

'Al Toomey! He works for you, doesn't he?'

'Toomey — yeah, he's on my books. But he's a no-account idler who doesn't know what a hard day's work is. What's with Toomey?'

'What is he supposed to be doing for you today?' Starrett demanded.

Satterfield grimaced. 'How in hell should I know? He was helping out at the general store but sloped off this morning and ain't been seen since. If his past record is anything to go by then he's on a drunk, and won't be back in circulation until he's sobered up. It happens that he's on his last warning about absenting himself. Now he'll be out of a job.'

'He's face down across a saddle outside the law office,' Starrett said quietly, and recounted the action that had taken place at Circle B earlier.

'So you're gonna lay the blame for his trouble at my door, huh?' Satterfield demanded.

'Like I said, I'm holding you responsible for everything that happens around here. You're riding the big saddle, Satterfield, and so you carry the can, and if you haven't got an explanation for Toomey's part in that raid this morning then I'm gonna throw you in jail until you can come up with a reasonable explanation.'

'You're loco if you think you can make this stick.' Satterfield stared at Starrett, his eyes glinting with fury. 'I'm a businessman and I've got thousands of dollars tied up in this town. I employ most of the men living around here. It's unreasonable to expect me to know where any one of my employees is at a given time. If you're gonna try and ride rough-shod over me then think again. I won't stand for that, and I've got powerful friends. You must know that money talks.'

'None of that cuts any ice with me,' Starrett said sharply. 'I'm giving you a warning, Satterfield. Pull in your horns or it will go bad for you. I'm here to clean up, and no one will stand in my way.'

'Talk is cheap.' Satterfield sneered, and Starrett smiled.

'You think so, huh? OK, you hang on to that attitude and we'll talk some more after the smoke clears — if you're still standing. You might own the town, but you don't own the folks living in it. I'm here to see that they get a fair crack of the whip. And after this you better keep your pet gunnies out of town or you'll run short of hired guns. You got any questions before I leave? I've laid it out straight, and that's the way it is gonna be.'

'I got nothing to say to you.' Satterfield spoke through clenched teeth. 'I'll be sending a man for the county sheriff, and then we'll see who is holding the whiphand.'

Starrett nodded and departed. He kept his hand close to the butt of his pistol as he went out to the street. He shouldered through the batwings to find a small, slightly built man standing over the body of Bat Rankin. There were six townsmen standing in a cluster in the background, looking in shocked silence at the dead gunman.

'I'm Joe Peck, the undertaker,' the small man said. 'Do you want me to take care of this body?'

'Yeah, and there's likely to be a good trade for you in the near future,' Starrett said. 'Take care of Al Toomey as well. He's across that horse outside the law office. I'm expecting a wagon to come in from Circle B, and it will be carrying a dozen dead men who made the mistake of trying to raid Bellamy's place this morning. When the wagon shows up you could try to identify the dead men. I'll be interested to know who they are, what they were doing out at Circle B, and if they have any friends in town.'

A ripple of excitement ran through the watching townsmen, and some of the men turned and hurried along the street to view Toomey's body.

'Do you know Toomey worked for

Satterfield?' Peck asked.

'Sure. I've spoken to Satterfield about that.' Starrett glanced around the street as he spoke, and saw two men emerging from the general store. One of the men was carrying a double-barrelled shotgun. The other was wearing crossed cartridge belts around his waist with twin pistols in tied-down holsters.

'Who are those men? Starrett demanded.

Peck glanced over his shoulder and started visibly. 'Hell, they are big trouble, Ranger. Ben Grover runs the store for Satterfield, and Hank Myhill is another of Satterfield's hired guns. It sure looks like they are loaded for bear and coming for you.'

'It's my job to face men like them,' Starrett said. He dropped a hand to his pistol and waited stoically for the two men to arrive.

7

The two men approached alertly, their faces taut and eyes narrowed. Grover, the storekeeper, was big and fleshy. The twin muzzles of the shotgun he was carrying were pointing at the ground, but his right index finger was caressing the triggers of the deadly weapon. Myhill was tall and thin, like a beanpole. Both his hands were down at his sides, and he looked to be on a hairspring, ready to flow into action at the drop of a hat. But his eagerness faded when he saw the Ranger badge on Starrett's chest. He moved his hands away from the butts of his holstered guns.

'Who in hell are you, stranger?' Myhill demanded. 'Did you kill Rankin?'

'He did, and from an even break,' one of the townsmen cut in. 'Rankin was the fastest around here, but he never stood a chance.'

'Does Satterfield know about this? Grover asked.

'I told him,' Starrett said. 'And he knows now that any more trouble around here will be down to him and he'll have to answer to the law for it. So what's on your minds, huh? Do you have any orders to follow Rankin?'

Both men gazed at Starrett as if he was a new species of rattlesnake. Grover removed his finger from the triggers of the shotgun and lowered the weapon until the muzzles were digging into the dust of the street. He leaned on the butt as if his legs suddenly refused to take his weight.

'I ain't likely to stand up to a Ranger,' Grover said, and let the shotgun fall to the ground. 'Count me out.'

Myhill expelled his pent-up breath in a long sigh. 'I'll talk to Mr Satterfield,' he said.

'Get rid of your hardware before you move,' Starrett told him in a flat tone. He was calm and ready for action, his right hand close to the butt of his holstered gun.

'Sure.' Myhill unbuckled his belts and let them fall to the ground. He stepped clear of them and went into the saloon.

'I need a drink,' Grover said. 'You got any objections, Ranger?'

'You can go about your lawful business,' Starrett said. 'Just be careful you don't overstep the line.'

Grover entered the saloon and Starrett turned slowly to survey the street. It was becoming crowded now, as townsfolk emerged from the buildings. Most of the men were armed, and Starrett had no idea how many were paid to fight for Satterfield. He saw Doc Bannerman emerge from the law office and walked along the street to meet him. Bannerman handed over the cell keys.

'Millett won't be thinking of moving out for a week or so,' Bannerman said. 'Am I needed along the street?'

'No. That's a job for the undertaker.

Bat Rankin wasn't as fast as he thought.'

'Does Satterfield know you've killed his top gun?'

'I have acquainted him with the fact.'

'You've made a good start, but it will be a lot harder to maintain your progress. I'll be at home if I'm needed again.'

'Thanks, Doc.' Starrett turned as he caught the sound of an approaching wagon and saw Toke Bellamy riding along the street beside a wagon. Two of the Circle B outfit were seated on the wagon. 'Wait a moment, Doc,' Starrett said. 'There might be some wounded men in that wagon.'

Starrett saw Bellamy ride into the sidewalk where Rankin was lying. The rancher sat his mount for some moments, gazing at the dead man. Then he came on at a canter to where Starrett was standing with the doctor.

'Did you kill Rankin?' Bellamy demanded.

'Sure! I'm the law around here now,'

Starrett replied. 'I've taken over. It's not the way I wanted to handle this chore, but that's how the cards have been dealt, and I'm happy to go along with that.'

'Starrett, my outfit will back you up if you need them,' Bellamy said. 'Doc, there are two men in the wagon still breathing. Will you take a look at them?'

Bannerman nodded, waited for the wagon to stop in front of the law office, and then climbed into the vehicle.

'Get the dead men out and give me some room in which to work,' he called, and Bellamy motioned to his two men.

'Stretch them out in front of the office,' Starrett said. 'I want the townsfolk to get a good look at them.' He turned to the men standing around the horse carrying the body of Al Toomey. 'You can give a hand here,' he instructed. 'Unload that wagon.'

He stood with Bellamy while the wagon was unloaded. The townsmen crowded around, studying dead faces,

164

but no one volunteered any information. Doc Bannerman worked on the two wounded men in silence and Starrett watched him. Bellamy nudged him, and pointed along the street when Starrett looked round.

'You got visitors,' Bellamy observed, and Starrett saw two Mexican riders coming into town at a trot. 'Heck, that tall, lean Mexican is Don Emilio Alvarez,' Bellamy said. 'Now what the heck does he want? I ain't seen him this side of the border in ten years. He owns most of the range for miles across the border — and used to own a lot of the country this side in the old days. He's a bad enemy of Satterfield. I think Satterfield cheated him when he took over the town and started up the RS ranch to the north.'

'That sounds interesting,' Starrett commented.

He studied the two riders as they approached. The elder man was in his fifties, his thin face showing the effect of many summers under the hot

Mexican sun. His eyes were shaded by the wide brim of his sombrero, but they were keen, like a hawk's. He wore an ornate jacket, and Starrett caught a glimpse of a blue silk shirt underneath. His trousers were trimmed with black braid. A pistol was holstered around his waist. His black horse had the lines of a thoroughbred, and he rode it easily. He said something to his younger companion, and they came towards the wagon.

'Don Emilio,' Bellamy greeted, smiling broadly. 'I haven't had the pleasure of seeing you in ten years. What brings you across the border?'

'We have big trouble across the river,' Don Emilio replied, his dark eyes glinting, 'and I heard that it had spilled over the water to your side. I can see by the dead men here that my information was correct.'

'Have you got rustler trouble?' Bellamy asked.

'Much trouble by cattle thieves; and the man causing it is the one who is responsible for your losses. He has

166

organized a very large band of rustlers and is working hand in hand with someone this side of the border who is buying in Mexican cattle while pushing many steers across from this side.'

'I guess we know who you are talking about,' Bellamy said. 'Well, you have turned up at just the right time, Don Emilio. The Texas Rangers have become interested in what is going on around here, and this is Buck Starrett, who has made a good start in bringing law and order back to us. I guess you two ought to get together and see what you can come up with. Your rustler across the border is Luis Ramirez, huh?'

'He is the one.' Don Emilio's gaze was intense as he studied Starrett's rugged face. 'I think we could help each other, *señor*. I have no control over what happens here, and you cannot operate in Mexico, so Ramirez is using that situation for his own ends. But we should be able to work out a plan that will give us the chance of putting an end to this wholesale rustling. I could

167

work from my side of the border while you do what you have to from here. With a little luck we could get Ramirez between us and finish him off. He has caused much trouble for Mexico over the years, and it is time he was stopped.'

'I agree with you so far, Don Emilio,' Starrett said. 'And I'm beginning to think that the only way to beat Ramirez is to tackle him as you suggest, from both sides of the border. If we make the border dangerous for him then he will have nowhere to hide.'

'That is what I have in mind.' Don Emilio spoke eagerly. He glanced at the younger Mexican at his side. 'This is my son Miguel. He is keen to ride with Ramirez, and will pass on information about the future movements of the rustlers.'

Starrett looked critically at the young man, who would be no more than twenty years old. His face was thin and harshly set. A huge sombrero was pushed back on his head and he was wearing a white silk blouse with a pale blue *sarape* adorning his lean waist; the bottom of which reached down almost to his ornate Mexican spurs. The pearl-handled butt of a pistol protruded from beneath his *sarape*. He looked as if he had never done a day's work in his short life, and the thought of him joining the rustlers as an undercover agent brought a smile of disbelief to Starrett's lips.

'You think I am not man enough to handle the job of infiltrating the Ramirez gang?' Miguel asked coldly, interpreting Starrett's smile as a criticism. 'I have been associating with Luis Ramirez for several months. He thinks I am a rich man's son who seeks adventure and excitement. He also thought I was not serious, until I arranged for him to steal a herd of my father's cattle, and now Ramirez trusts me like a brother. I have told Don Emilio about Ramirez's plans, and now we need your help on this side of the border to spring a trap which will rid us of this scourge of rustling.'

'I like what you are saying.' Starrett nodded. 'Come into the office and we will talk tactics. I have only recently arrived here to start operating, and although I have made some progress I still have much to investigate before I can take firm action.'

He led the way into the law office and the two Mexicans followed closely. Bellamy accompanied them and closed the door to shut out the excited chatter of the men on the street. Starrett pulled forward chairs for his guests and then sat down behind the desk. He was interested in what Don Emilio had suggested, for he realized that he would be unable to end his assignment successfully without help from law-abiding men south of the border.

'Are you aware that Satterfield is linked with Ramirez?' Don Emilio asked. 'We cannot beat Ramirez if we do nothing about Satterfield. They will have to go together.'

'I'm certain Satterfield is guilty of

many illegal practices on both sides of the border,' Starrett said. 'I have made a start on loosening his grip on this town, but he is well dug in and it will take a lot of effort to remove him.'

'It is good that you have his measure.' Don Emilio nodded. 'It will be a simple matter to beat their set-up. We will lay a trap for Ramirez and lure Satterfield into Mexico, where we can deal with him.'

'I think Satterfield has more sense than to cross the border these days,' Bellamy said. 'He made his start in business driving wet-backs across the river. All we need to do in his case is get evidence of his guilty dealings and the Rangers will take care of him.'

'In that case my son will pursue his rustling activities with Ramirez until we can plan a trap and spring it.' Don Emilio nodded. 'All I need at this moment is your assurance that you will act with us when we ask for your help.'

'I'll go along with that, Don Emilio.' Starrett nodded.

'Starrett, if I have your word that the law will back anything I do to help Don Emilio then I'll pull out all the stops to help him,' Bellamy cut in eagerly. 'I could handle the business as a go-between on the border because you'll have your hands full around here with Satterfield. You'll need to get some more Rangers into the county, and with my outfit doing its share, we should prove to be more than a match for Ramirez.'

'It will not be easy,' Don Emilio mused. 'Ramirez is like a wolf. He seems to be able to sniff out traps and avoid them, or turn them to his advantage.'

Starrett nodded. 'I'll make some arrangements at this end, and we'll be ready to ride against Ramirez the moment you get word to us.'

Don Emilio arose and held out his hand. Starrett shook hands, pleased with the way the situation was evolving. There was an air of determination about Don Emilio which augured well for the future. Bellamy was smiling, and Starrett knew enough about the rancher to accept that he was happy with Don Emilio's intervention.

'I'm heading back to Circle B, Don Emilio,' Bellamy said as the Mexicans prepared to leave. 'Perhaps I can have the pleasure of your company as far as the border. If Satterfield gets word that you are here in town he may try to take advantage of the situation and attack you before you get back to Mexico.'

'I am touched by your concern for my safety, Señor Bellamy,' Don Emilio replied, and a faint smile touched his thin lips. 'I did take the precaution of bringing an escort of ten guns with me and they are waiting just outside town. However I'd welcome your company as far as your ranch. We have some small details to consider before we go our separate ways.'

Starrett followed his visitors out to the street and Bellamy again offered the services of some of his crew to help maintain law and order in the town. Starrett declined, and watched the Circle B outfit ride out with Don

Emilio and his son. He turned his attention to the activity in front of the law office and found the undertaker, Joe Peck — who looked like an oversized crow in his long back frock coat — surveying the dead men with a practised eye.

'Get what details you can about these men before you bury them,' Starrett instructed Peck.

'There are a couple I know by sight,' Peck volunteered. 'That big man in the blue shirt, Bud Hooper. I've seen him around town. He was friendly with Ike Benson, the carpenter, and that little guy down at the end — his name is Pete Mayhew. He's been hanging around with Rafe Millett.'

'Is that a fact? Thanks for the information. Get these bodies off the street soon as you can, huh?'

Peck nodded. 'Who is gonna pick up the tab for burying these galoots?'

'The town, of course,' Starrett replied. 'Leave it to me.'

'I don't care who forks out, so long as

I get paid.' Peck turned away but Starrett stopped him.

'Have you any idea where Ike Benson is working today?' he queried.

'Sure. He was fixing the back door of the general store earlier. Seems someone tried to break into the place last night. Grover was in a sweat about it because Satterfield chewed him out for not taking proper precautions.'

'Thanks.' Starrett looked around the street before moving on. He spotted Ben Grover standing in the open doorway of the store looking intently at the scene in front of the law office.

Grover scowled when Starrett paused in front of him. He turned abruptly and stepped back into the store. Starrett followed him closely, and the big storekeeper halted and swung around, his hands clenching into fists.

'You want something?' Grover demanded.

'Sure. I need to talk to Ike Benson. He's working on your back door, huh?'

'Yeah, but don't stop him or that

door will never get fixed.'

Starrett walked around Grover and started through the store towards the back door. Grover reached out a big paw and grasped Starrett's left arm.

'Not through my store,' he declared. 'If you wanta talk to Benson then go down the alley.'

Starrett glanced down at Grover's hand. 'Get your hand off me or I'll break your arm,' he said quietly.

Grover released his hold quickly. 'What kind of a law man are you, talking that way?' he demanded. 'If you fancy yourself you've only got to take off that law badge you're wearing and we'll try conclusions.'

'Any time I'm not so busy,' Starrett responded, 'I'll bear your offer in mind.'

Grover followed closely as Starrett walked through the store to the private quarters at the rear. He stood within earshot when Starrett reached the slight figure of Ike Benson, who was working on the lock of the back door. Starrett glanced pointedly at Grover.

'I don't need your presence,' he said. 'When I've finished here I'll go back to the street by the alley, so beat it. If Satterfield told you to try and make life difficult for me then you better watch your step or you'll find yourself behind bars.'

A faint grin touched Grover's fleshy lips and he turned away without further comment. Starrett turned to Benson, who was regarding him in some alarm.

'So you're a Ranger!' Benson observed, his blue eyes blinking nervously. 'I heard there was someone in town making life difficult for folk.'

'Only for those who break the law,' Starrett responded.

'I can't tell you who tried to break in here. I only do the repairs.'

'I'm interested in Bud Hooper. He works with you, I hear.'

'Sometimes, but he ain't been around today. What's your interest in him?'

'I need to find out what he's been doing recently.'

'Why don't you ask him?'

'I can't — he's dead.'

Benson's face paled, and his mouth gaped in shock. 'Dead?' he repeated in a hollow tone. 'What in hell happened to him?'

Starrett explained, and Benson's shock deepened.

'Heck, I could tell by how he talked that he didn't care how he made his dough, but to go raiding Circle B!' Benson broke off, shaking his head.

'I'd like to know who would pay Hooper and those others to raid Bellamy's ranch,' Starrett said.

'I can't help you there! Hooper didn't talk much about his business. But you should talk to Mary Dent. Hooper was shacked up with her. She lives in a place just past the Kenton guest house, and helps Martha Kenton with cleaning and cooking.'

'Thanks. I'll check with her.'

Starrett turned away and entered the alley beside the store. He went back to the street and paused in the alley mouth to check his surroundings. Joe

Peck and his assistant were pushing a hand cart containing three bodies along the street to the mortuary. There was still a crowd standing in front of the law office although some of the men were beginning to drift away. Starrett looked to his right, towards Satterfield's saloon, and his expression hardened when he saw Satterfield standing at the batwings of the saloon in the company of two tough-looking, heavily armed men. Two horses were standing at the tie-rail in front of the saloon, and looked as if they had recently travelled fast. It looked to Starrett as though Satterfield was giving explicit instructions to the two newcomers, and he needed no stretch of the imagination to believe those orders concerned him.

He guessed it was time Satterfield struck back at the man causing him trouble, and Starrett was expecting trouble because a man of Satterfield's ilk, who held his business together with fear and violence, could not afford to let opposition grow unchecked. There would be a number of men in the community who appeared to go along with the situation but would step out of line if someone came on the scene to lead their resistance. Starrett knew he would be a prime target for Satterfield's fight-back.

He was tempted to confront Satterfield and discover what the big man had in mind, but he turned in the opposite direction and went along the street to the law office. The crowd was thinning considerably — most of the men heading towards the saloon. They were talking excitedly about the situation, and Starrett was aware that he came under considerable scrutiny. But no one spoke to him, and he noticed that most of the men averted their gaze when he looked directly at them, as if afraid he would start asking embarrassing questions.

Starrett grasped the arm of one man and halted him in mid-stride. The man turned an intense gaze upon him, like a startled jack-rabbit.

'I don't bite!' Starrett commented. 'Just tell me where Mary Dent lives.'

'See that house with the white shutters?' the man answered quickly. 'That's the Kenton guest house. Mary Dent lives in the second house past it.'

Starrett nodded and the man hurried away. Starrett glanced back along the street and saw Satterfield pointing in his direction while talking swiftly to the two hardcases. He went along the street past the guest house and paused outside Mary Dent's home. A woman was peering out of a front window from behind a dingy curtain, but withdrew her head swiftly when Starrett opened the gate and walked to the front door.

There was no reply when he knocked loudly, and Starrett waited patiently until he assumed that the woman had no intention of answering his summons. He tried the door, found it unlocked, and opened it slightly.

'Hello, Mary Dent,' he called. 'I'd like a word with you.'

There was no immediate reply. Starrett contained his impatience and thrust the door open wider. He stepped into the house, and when he opened the first door on the right he was confronted by the woman who had peered out of the window. She seemed scared. Her attractive face was pale and her hands shook as she half-held them out towards him, as if hoping to ward off bad news.

'I'm sorry to trouble you but if you are Mary Dent then I need to talk to you.'

'If you've come to talk about Bud then I can't tell you anything,' she said nervously. 'He never told me about his business. Go talk to Bud. He's working with Ike Benson today.'

'I've talked to Benson, who says he hasn't seen Bud. I'm afraid I've got some bad news, Mary. Bud is dead. He was shot earlier today out at Circle B in the company of a dozen men who attacked the ranch.'

Mary uttered a cry and buried her

face in her hands. Starrett gave her some moments while she sobbed. It was not often that he hated his job, but this was one of the times when he wished he had chosen a different career.

8

'I'm sorry to bother you at a time like this, Mary,' Starrett said quietly. 'But I need to ask you some questions about Bud. Can you tell me what he was doing with a bunch of men acting against the law? They shot up Circle B.'

'I don't know.' Mary pressed her hands to her face. 'Bud never spoke about anything. I can't talk to you now. I must go to Martha at the guest house. I work there.'

'I'll take you,' Starrett suggested. 'But first we must talk about Bud.'

'All I can tell you is that he worked for Red Satterfield, doing different jobs. He could turn his hand to most things. He was a good man. He didn't drink much and never caused any trouble.'

'But he was killed in the act of shooting up Circle B. Tell me about his friends. Who did he mix with?'

'I wouldn't know any of them. We never went out together. He worked around town and I work at the guest house. I only ever saw him when we were both home.'

'OK.' Starrett could tell he was going to learn absolutely nothing. 'I'll talk to you some more when you've got over your shock. I'll see you to the guest house now.'

'I can manage alone,' Mary replied, shaking her head. 'I need to collect myself before seeing anyone.'

She burst into tears and buried her face in her hands. Starrett gazed at her for a moment and then departed silently. He paused on the street to check his surroundings. Satterfield was still standing in front of the saloon but there was no sign of the two hardcases who had been with him, and Starrett's hard gaze probed the street, looking for their whereabouts. But they were nowhere in sight, and their horses were gone.

Had they ridden out of town or taken

their mounts to the livery barn? Starrett knew he had to find them before turning his attention elsewhere. He entered a passage between two houses, headed for the back lots, and hurried to an alley opposite the livery barn where he remained in cover while subjecting the barn to a close scrutiny. There was no sign of movement at the stable and he waited for the two hardcases to appear. When his patience faded he crossed the street and entered the barn.

The gloomy interior of the stable was hushed. Starrett turned towards the office. He caught the mumble of voices coming from it and crossed to the door, his right hand resting on the butt of his holstered pistol. When he looked into the office he drew his gun instantly, for Kenton was seated at his desk with a hardcase standing over him. The man, one of those Starrett had seen talking to Satterfield, was holding a gun on Kenton.

'What's going on here?' Starrett demanded.

The sound of his voice jerked the hardcase into action. He swung his pistol towards Starrett who triggered a shot that blasted out the silence. The slug struck the man in the right shoulder, causing him to drop his weapon as he fell back against the rear wall of the office. The barn rocked to the hammering shot, then the echoes faded slowly.

Joe Kenton got to his feet. His face was pale. He rubbed his chin as he gazed at Starrett.

'I'm sure glad to see you,' he declared. 'Wiskin was fixing to kill me.'

Starrett covered the fallen man although he was in no condition to resist.

'So what is this all about?' Starrett demanded. 'Do you know this man, Joe?'

'Yeah, he's no stranger,' Kenton shrugged. 'This is Abe Wiskin. He rides for Satterfield out at the RS spread.'

'He was talking to Satterfield in front of the saloon a few minutes ago,'

Starrett mused, 'and there was another hardcase with him. When I saw them I figured Satterfield was planning to set them on to me, but one of them came here for you, so it looks like Satterfield set you up. I need to find that second man.'

'Wiskin never rides anywhere without Matt Fuller.' Kenton shook his head. 'It doesn't look too good. Satterfield must be getting tired of the way I stand out against him at every turn. I'm gonna have to watch my step in future.' He picked up the gun dropped by Wiskin. 'We'll have to find Fuller. Maybe Satterfield sent him after you, so I'll walk along to the law office with you. I guess you're gonna jail Wiskin, huh?'

'Yeah, and then I'll have another talk with Satterfield. My job around here will be easier if he's out of circulation.' Starrett reached down, grasped Wiskin by the uninjured shoulder and dragged him to his feet. The man swayed, and would have fallen if Starrett had not supported him. 'Let's go,' Starrett ordered. 'I'll fetch the doctor to you when you're behind bars.'

They left the office and Kenton walked to a stall where two horses were tied.

'Those two broncs were outside the saloon when Satterfield was talking to the two men,' Starrett said.

'Yeah, the brown horse belongs to Wiskin and Fuller rides that grey. You're gonna have to pull in Fuller before you do anything else, Starrett. If he's laying for you he'll shoot you in the back at the first opportunity. That's the kind of man he is.'

'I'll get around to him,' Starrett replied grimly.

They left the barn. Starrett was surprised to see townsfolk already hurrying along the street, attracted by the gunshot. He was expecting trouble from any of Satterfield's men but they reached the law office without incident. Kenton went to fetch Doc Bannerman while Starrett lodged Wiskin in a cell. Millett, lying on the bunk in the adjoining cell, lifted his head and gazed without interest at the new prisoner.

'So what orders did Satterfield give you, Wiskin?' Starrett demanded. 'I saw you and Fuller talking to him in front of the saloon. You better loosen up and come clean about what's going on.'

Wiskin ignored the question, stretched out on the bunk in his cell and closed his eyes. His face held a sullen expression and his lips were compressed against his teeth. Starrett shrugged, aware of the kind of man he was up against.

'OK, if that's the way you want to play it,' he said. 'I've got all the time in the world.'

'If I know Satterfield then you've got no time left,' Millett interjected.

Starrett grinned at the deputy and went through to the front office to await the doctor.

Within minutes Joe Kenton returned with Bannerman.

'I've got those two wounded men Bellamy brought in at my place,' Bannerman said. 'One looks like he'll be dead before morning. The other, Jack Keller, is in a bad way, but he should pull through. I've seen him around town a time or two. I think he rides for Satterfield out at the RS ranch. You'd do well to ask Satterfield about him.'

'I'll do that,' Starrett promised.

Bannerman went into the cells to attend the wounded man. Starrett intended leaving Kenton in the law office while he went along the street to the saloon, but with Fuller loose in town he dared not risk Kenton's life further.

'You'll make a complaint about Wiskin, huh?' he asked Kenton.

'You bet I will.' Kenton's expression showed determination. 'The situation around here has got too much for most of the folk not in Satterfield's pocket and it's time we stood up to be counted. I'll make a statement about what happened, and if you can throw Satterfield in a cell then so much the better, but taking him in might light the fuse to a powder keg. Satterfield has got a big outfit out at the RS ranch which is bossed by a tough gun hand, Trig Wyatt, and you can bet Wyatt will show up here with a dozen hardcases to bust Satterfield loose the minute he hears you've jailed him. So you'd better be ready to fight big odds.'

'I follow the letter of the law,' Starrett said firmly. 'Anyone stepping out of line will be arrested and charged. That's my job, and I'll do it to the best of my ability while I am able. That's the way it works, Joe, regardless of odds, and I will get to the bottom of what's going on around here. You can count on that.'

'Here in town it won't be so difficult.' Kenton frowned as he considered. 'Satterfield has about half a dozen tough men around who run things for him — men like Grover and Hank Myhill — and they are always ready to gang up on any opposition, so if you can jail Satterfield and keep him behind bars you'll cut the head off the monster and won't get much trouble around town. But be ready for big trouble when the RS outfit gets wind of what you're doing here. They'll hit town like a thunderstorm, and you'll be up to your neck in it.'

'I'll confront Satterfield now,' Starrett said, 'and arrest him if I can find evidence of his wrongdoing. Will you stay here locked in the office until I get back? I wouldn't want Fuller coming in here while I'm absent and springing Wiskin.'

'I'll stand by,' Kenton said. 'You go and do what you have to do.'

Starrett nodded. 'I'll leave by the back door,' he mused. 'Fuller might be on the street waiting to draw a bead on me. I'll look him up as soon as I've put Satterfield behind bars. Come and lock the back door behind me, Joe.'

He left the jail and walked along the back lots to the rear of the saloon. The afternoon was well past and the sun was in the western quarter of the brassy sky. He experienced a pang of hunger and wondered when he would get an opportunity to eat. He tried the back door of the saloon, found it locked, and grimaced. So he would have to do this the hard way — enter through the batwings in the bar and confront any set-up which Satterfield might have prepared.

Starrett traversed the alley on the far side of the saloon and walked to the street end. He paused at a side window roughly halfway along the alley to take a look into the big bar room. The place was deserted; only the bartender was inside, wiping down the polished bar. Starrett's eyes glinted when he saw a double-barrelled shotgun lying close to the bartender's hand. He was about to go on when he spotted a man standing under the flight of stairs leading to the upper storey. He was watching the batwings intently. The man was Grover, and he was holding a pistol in his right hand.

The saloon was otherwise devoid of life. Starrett suppressed a sigh and went on to check the street. He needed to know the whereabouts of Fuller before he tried to overcome Satterfield's set-up. His experienced gaze took in every conceivable spot where trouble might be waiting, probing the shadows in the alleys along the street. He saw nothing suspicious, and dropped his right hand to the butt of his holstered gun as he decided to enter the saloon and spring Satterfield's gun trap.

Starrett was uneasy because there was no sign of Fuller around the street, but then he did not expect the gunman to advertise his position. The street itself looked strangely deserted, and Starrett felt a prickling in the short hairs on the back of his neck as he checked the scene again for anything he might have missed. When he saw the barrel of a rifle poking out through an open window in the hotel he caught his breath and squinted his eyes, wondering just how many more of Satterfield's men were in cover around the area with ready guns.

He drew a long breath and held it as

he eased out of the alley mouth and walked to the batwings of the saloon. He wanted Satterfield, and there was only one way to get the man. He pushed through the swing doors and stepped to his left. The batwings creaked, and the 'tender swung round to face them, his right hand reaching out for the shotgun.

'Don't pick it up,' Starrett warned. His gaze flickered to the flight of stairs where he had seen Grover waiting. The man was no longer there. 'Where is Grover?' he demanded.

'I ain't seen him.' The bartender's voice was high-pitched with tension. 'He ain't been around at all today.'

'You're lying. I saw him standing under the stairs a minute ago when I looked through the side window. Try again, and this time come up with the truth.'

'He went into Mr Satterfield's office.' The bartender glanced at the nearby shotgun but made no effort to reach for it, although Starrett had not drawn his pistol.

'So we'll go to the office.' Starrett drew his gun with a fast movement, and the bartender blinked. 'You lead the way, and keep your mouth shut.'

The bartender came out from behind the bar and walked to the door of Satterfield's office. He paused when he reached it and glanced enquiringly at Starrett.

'Open it,' Starrett hissed, closing in. He thrust the bartender headlong into the office as the door swung wide.

The bartender sprawled forward on to his hands and knees. Starrett moved in, gun levelled. Satterfield was seated behind his desk, Grover was standing in front of him. Both men jerked their attention towards the door, and froze at the sight of Starrett's ominous figure and levelled gun.

'What the hell is going on?' Satterfield demanded.

'I'm hoping you can tell me,' Starrett replied. 'You were talking to Wiskin and Fuller in front of the saloon some time ago, and then I stopped Wiskin from assaulting Joe Kenton. I'm arresting you, Satterfield, on suspicion of planning assault or murder, so get up and come with me. You're gonna see the inside of the jail.'

'You can't arrest me!' Satterfield's blue eyes filled with alarm. 'If I don't attend to my business then nothing gets done around here, and nobody gets paid.'

'Don't tell me what my duty is,' Starrett said firmly, 'especially when I've got my gun in my hand. Just do like I tell you and we'll get this done real easy. Stand up and get rid of any hardware you're carrying. You too, Grover. I'm putting you behind bars. Where is Fuller, Satterfield?'

'I told him and Wiskin to go back to the ranch,' Satterfield said through his teeth. 'I don't want any trouble around here until I'm ready to handle it. I wouldn't buck the law under any circumstance because I couldn't stay in business long if I tried that. You need to ignore the talk about me going around town. None of it is true.'

'Is that why you had the local law in your back pocket?' Starrett demanded. 'I guess you must be missing Millett now he's in jail. Stand up and get moving.'

Satterfield got to his feet. 'I've got a .41 Derringer in my right pocket,' he said, moving his hand cautiously.

'Take it out slow and throw it on your desk,' Starrett said. He waited until Satterfield had complied, then he motioned to Grover. 'Get rid of your gun, Grover.'

The storekeeper eased his pistol out of its holster and dropped it on the floor.

'Are you jailing me?' the bartender demanded.

Starrett considered the man and then shook his head. 'No. But you better watch your step if you want to stay out of the calaboose. Come on, Satterfield, let's get this done. I got other things to handle before the sun goes down.'

Satterfield came around the desk and

walked to the door. He paused and glanced back at the motionless bartender.

'Charlie, go tell Tricker what's happened here,' he instructed.

'Who is Tricker?' Starrett demanded.

'Vince Tricker, my attorney.' Satterfield scowled. 'He'll make you change your mind pretty damn quick about jailing me.'

'Don't bet on it,' Starrett retorted. 'You know where the jail is so go ahead, and don't even think about giving me any trouble.'

Satterfield, followed closely by Grover, walked out of the office with Starrett behind them, a gun in his hand. They left the saloon and walked along the street towards the law office. Starrett watched his surroundings, wondering where Fuller had got to. He expected the gunman to make a play at any time, but they reached the office without trouble, and Joe Kenton, holding a shotgun, unlocked the door when Starrett called out to be admitted.

'So you've finally come out into the

open against me, Joe,' Satterfield observed. 'I guess I'll know what to do about you when I get out of here. If you've got any sense at all you'll hop on a horse and ride hell for leather for other parts before I'm turned loose.'

'Empty your pockets on the desk,' Starrett ordered. 'And you, Grover. You might think you're gonna get out of here, Satterfield, but I've got different ideas about that.'

He checked both prisoners before ushering them into the cell block. Millett stood at the door of his cell, his fleshy face showing shock at the turn of events, but he said nothing, and Starrett locked Satterfield and Grover in a cell. He studied Satterfield's harsh face for a moment before speaking.

'I've just learned that another of your employees was out breaking the law today, Satterfield. First it was Toomey and then Jack Keller.'

'What are you talking about?' Satterfield demanded. 'I never heard of Jack Keller. Who in hell is he?'

'He was one of your riders at your ranch.' Starrett spoke in a quiet, deliberate tone.

'Is that so?' Satterfield smiled. 'Then you'll have to talk to my ranch foreman, Trig Wyatt. He does all the hiring and firing. I wouldn't know the names of half the men on the payroll. Wyatt runs the spread, and I stay well away from it while he shows a profit each year.'

'I'll certainly talk to Wyatt,' Starrett promised.

'What has Keller done that's against the law?' Satterfield demanded.

Starrett explained, and saw shock appear on Satterfield's face.

'If that's a fact then I'll be talking to Wyatt myself,' Satterfield said.

'Are you saying you know nothing about the activities of the two men in question?' Starrett shook his head. 'Using ignorance as a defence against criminal charges won't stand up in court. You'll have to do a lot better than that. You will be facing some serious charges.'

'I've got more to do than keep an eye on the men on my payroll. I pay foremen and managers to do that, so if some of the men I employ are criminals then go for the men who hired them.' Satterfield turned away, sat down on the bunk in the cell, and folded his arms.

Starrett regarded the man for a moment and then went back into the office. Kenton was seated at the desk, polishing the twin barrels of the shotgun and looking uneasy.

'I've come out on your side after years of worrying and waiting,' Kenton said, 'and I'm thinking I might have made my move too early. You are alone against Satterfield's set-up and I wouldn't bet on you with anyone's money. How do you expect to fight twenty tough gun hands when they come rattling into town?'

'I guess I'll have to try and stay one jump ahead of them,' Starrett replied. 'You can pull out now if you wish, Joe. I'm going to look for Fuller.'

A knock sounded at the door.

Kenton started nervously, then put down the shotgun and drew his pistol.

'I'll get it.' Starrett walked to the street door, unbolted it and jerked it open. His right hand was close to the butt of his holstered gun as he looked into the smooth, fleshy face of a small man dressed in a brown store suit and wearing a flat-brimmed Plains hat. 'Who are you?' Starrett demanded, although he could guess at the newcomer's occupation.

'Vincent Tricker, attorney-at-law,' the man replied pompously. 'I understand you have a client of mine, Frank Satterfield, in jail. I'd like to talk to him. I'll need a rundown on the charges against him and I will arrange bail for him.'

'Satterfield is behind bars and will stay where he is until I have checked out the facts behind his arrest,' Starrett said firmly, disliking Tricker at first sight. 'If I find he has charges to answer then nothing you can do will spring him loose, so don't start spouting the law at me.'

'I would like to see my client,' Tricker

said in an ominously quiet tone, 'and I would advise you to be very careful in your decisions regarding Mr Satterfield. He is a man of great importance in this community, and if you handle him wrongly then you could find yourself in a bad legal situation.'

'So what's new?' Starrett demanded. 'You'll make an effort to have me kicked out of my job, huh? Now that's a frightening prospect. Let me tell you something. I'm short-handed here at the moment and I've got a lot to do so I don't have the time to stand around while you try to cook up some way of springing Satterfield out of jail. Get out of here and try your luck again later.'

'You can't treat me like this!' Tricker exclaimed.

Starrett closed the door in the lawyer's face and shot home the bolt. He turned to find Kenton shaking his head.

'I figure that was a bad move, Starrett. Tricker could make a lot of trouble for you.'

'I'll risk that. Like I said — right now I've got things to do. Satterfield will stay behind bars at least until tomorrow morning, and in that time I hope to strengthen the law in this town. I'm worried about you, Joe. Satterfield has made a threat against you, and he could get word to any of his men in town to take care of you. So how's about you riding out to Circle B and telling Bellamy I could do with three or four good men in here to back me? That would be a big help, and the trip will keep you out of the way.'

'I'll do that,' Kenton replied without hesitation. 'But what will you do while I'm away? Your life could be in worse danger than mine. If Satterfield can get rid of you his trail will be clear again.'

'I'll stick around here and make sure nobody tries to bust Satterfield loose.'

'I'll ride hell for leather,' Kenton promised. 'Bellamy will send his whole outfit in here to back you, but it will be some hours before I can get back.'

Starrett nodded and led Kenton to

the back door. He watched the stableman head off to the livery barn before closing and locking the door. He was content with the situation. He could hold the jail against all comers until hell froze over, and he set about making preparations to fight off any attack that might develop.

He checked all the weapons in the office, loaded the rifles and shotguns in the rack on the back wall, and checked the supply of ammunition, satisfying himself that he had sufficient to fight anything Satterfield's gunmen might try against him. He opened the door between the office and the cells and prowled around the interior of the building as night closed in and shadows thickened in the corners. He was hungry, but dared not leave the jail, aware that there would be time later to eat, when some of the Circle B outfit arrived.

From time to time he studied the street from the big front window of the office, but saw no movement anywhere outside, and did not know if that was a good sign or not. He could not relax his vigilance and when night settled he remained in the close darkness, silent and deadly, ready to flow into action at the first sign of trouble.

Later, he heard the sound of hoofs along the street. He drew his pistol and pressed close to the big window in an attempt to see movement. Shortly, two riders appeared and dismounted outside the office. Starrett watched from the shadows as the two men approached the office door.

'Declare yourselves,' he called when a heavy hand pounded on the door.

'Is that you, Starrett?' a voice answered. 'It's Spencer and Lunt out here. We tracked the bunch that hit Circle B earlier. Let us in and we'll tell you about it.'

Starrett heaved a sigh of relief and unbolted the street door. It looked like his lonely vigil was at an end.

9

Spencer and Lunt entered the office and paused on the threshold, unable to see in the inky blackness. Lunt struck a match and shielded it with his hand as he walked to the desk to light the lamp standing on it. Starrett blinked to accustom his eyes to the yellow glare.

'What's going on?' Spencer demanded.

'I've been expecting an attack.' Starrett explained the events that had taken place since his return from Circle B. The punchers glanced at each other when Satterfield's arrest was mentioned.

'You really got Red Satterfield behind bars?' Spencer demanded.

'No wonder you were expecting to be attacked,' Lunt added. 'Just wait until word gets out to the RS outfit. Trig Wyatt will show up with the whole bunch, and those guys are always loaded for bear.'

'So where did the tracks of those men who hit Circle B lead to?' Starrett demanded.

'A run-down place that once belonged to Pete Cash,' Spencer said. 'Cash was murdered a couple of years back. His killer was never caught and the spread lay derelict after Pete's death. It borders Satterfield's place, and his outfit have kind of taken it over. We followed those tracks the raiders left and they went right into the yard of Cash's place. We didn't go in to look around because several more hardcases are there.'

'Bellamy brought in the survivors of those raiders,' Starrett said. 'Two were still alive, and Doc Bannerman checked them out. He named one of them as Jack Keller, who rides for RS.'

'Toomey was one of those killed at Circle B this morning, and he also worked for Satterfield,' Spencer mused. 'It sure looks like Satterfield's got his finger in a big pie.'

'Is this the first time you've been able to tie Satterfield's outfit in with the trouble Circle B has been experiencing?' Starrett asked.

'We've had suspicions, but there's been nothing solid,' Lunt replied.

'But what happened today has kind of changed things, huh?' Spencer demanded. 'So what do we do now?'

'There is a hardcase called Matt Fuller somewhere around town,' Starrett said. 'He's got to be curbed. I'm waiting for some of your outfit to show up to guard my prisoners so I can look for Fuller. I also need to make arrangements for the prisoners to be fed, and I must get some cartridges from the store. If there is gonna be a showdown here in town then I've got to be ready to fight.'

'We can sit around in here while you go about your business,' Spencer offered.

'Sure,' Lunt agreed. 'But watch out for Fuller. He's a hard man.'

'My world is full of hard men,' Starrett observed. 'But if you think you can handle the job in here then I'll get moving. All you have to do is guard the place, and don't let in anyone you don't trust.'

'It sounds easy!' Spencer grinned and dropped a hand to the butt of his pistol.

Starrett smiled and prepared to leave. He selected a shotgun from the rack and stuffed cartridges for the double-barrelled weapon into his pockets.

'I'll leave by the back door,' he said, 'and I'll be back as soon as I've handled my chores.'

'Don't worry about this place,' Lunt assured him. 'It'll still be standing when you return.'

Starrett slipped out of the jail by the back door and stood in the dense shadows at the rear until his eyes became accustomed to the gloom. The town seemed quiet — too quiet, he thought. He moved slowly to the nearest alley and walked cautiously to the street end. The town seemed deserted. There were lights in some of the buildings, but no one was moving around. There was an air of quiet brooding hanging over the town and the many shadows seemed to be laced with hostility. Starrett wondered if the townsfolk knew something of which he was not aware.

He walked along the street, moving noiselessly, and his hard gaze checked the shadows as he eased towards the saloon. Matt Fuller had seemingly disappeared from the face of the earth. If he had been given orders to deal with the Ranger in town then he should have made a move before now, especially if he had seen Wiskin being jailed.

There were a dozen men in the saloon, Starrett observed, when he peered through the alley window. Most of them were standing at the bar, and Starrett studied them, looking for Fuller. He failed to spot the hardcase but saw Hank Myhill talking to the bartender. He assumed that Satterfield's men in town were waiting for gun help to arrive from the RS ranch before trying to redress the situation in Satterfield's favour.

Starrett did not enter the saloon. He wanted Fuller and the man was not there. He turned and began a round of the street. When he reached the general store he peered inside, wondering who was handling the business with Grover in jail. He saw a middle-aged woman and an older man clearing up before closing, and went in to pick up some extra ammunition.

The woman turned to Starrett when she heard his boots on the pine boards, and her smile of welcome faded when she saw the Ranger badge on his chest.

'When are you going to turn Mr Grover loose?' she demanded. 'He's got this place to run, and while you hold him in jail I have all the heavy work to do.'

'He may be inside for a long, long time,' Starrett replied. 'It all depends on what he's been doing around here. Give me three boxes of .45 cartridges and a couple of boxes of .44–40.'

'I don't know that I ought to sell you anything.' The woman glared at Starrett.

'I'll take what I want if you refuse to serve me,' Starrett replied.

The old man walked around the counter, picked up several boxes of shells and placed them before Starrett, who reached into his pocket for a sheaf of greenbacks. Starrett heard leather scrape on the threshold and glanced over his shoulder to see Fuller entering the store. The gunman was hawk-faced, his dark eyes filled with a hard glitter. Starrett turned to face him, his right hand down at his side, the shotgun in his left hand. Fuller halted and remained motionless, both hands hanging limply at his sides.

'I've been waiting for you to come out of the jail,' Fuller said. 'Now we'll go back there and turn Mr Satterfield and those others loose.'

Starrett shook his head. 'No dice!' he said. 'I've put Satterfield where he belongs, and he'll stay there until I say he can go. There's only one way you can get Satterfield out of that jail, Fuller. You have to go through me.'

Fuller clenched his hands and then relaxed them. He lifted his right hand until it hovered just above the butt of the pistol in his right-hand holster.

'I figured it was the only way,' he said, grinning, 'so get to it.'

Starrett remained motionless, watching the gunman intently. Fuller hesitated for several tense moments before starting his play, and then his hand moved like lightning. Starrett set his hand in motion simultaneously, and metal scraped leather as he grasped his pistol and drew it, cocking the weapon before it cleared leather. Fuller was fast. His gun began to lift, but Starrett fired before Fuller could draw a bead.

The quick gun blast rocked the store and echoes flew. Fuller took the slug in his chest and spun around to fall upon his face, his gun spilling from his hand. He hit the floor hard and did not move thereafter. A trickle of blood ran into a groove in the floor beside him.

Starrett slid his pistol back into its holster. His face was expressionless as he returned his attention to the man and the woman, who were frozen in shock, mouths gaping and fear in their eyes. Starrett threw some greenbacks on the counter and picked up the cartridges.

'Get Joe Peck to clear up this mess,' he rasped. 'I'll be in the law office if anyone around town wants me.'

He stepped over Fuller's body and departed into the shadows. The town was still quiet, but he knew the sound of the shot would bring men running, most of them loyal to Satterfield. He strode resolutely along the sidewalk back to the jail. Spencer and Lunt were standing in the open doorway of the office, their guns drawn. They backed into the office when Starrett crowded them.

'We heard the shot,' Spencer said. 'Did you get Fuller?'

'I had to kill him,' Starrett responded. 'It's all I can do now except wait for help to turn up. It looks like being a long night.'

He closed and bolted the street door and went to the desk.

'Maybe we can go out and get some grub,' Spencer said. 'It's been a long day for us, and we need to stoke up. Heck, my ribs are rattling against my spine. We ain't had a bite since breakfast this morning.'

'Sure,' Starrett said instantly. 'And bring me something to eat when you return. I'm plumb empty. The prisoners will have to wait until morning. I'm hoping some of your outfit will show up around midnight.'

Spencer and Lunt departed, and Starrett sat down at the desk and resigned himself to a long wait. He occupied the time considering the situation and came to the conclusion that all he could do was wait for help to arrive. If he managed to keep Satterfield and the others behind bars at least until morning then he had a good chance of smothering the trouble that had existed in this Devil's Outpost.

Thirty minutes passed like an age;

and the silence hanging over the town was like a shroud. Starrett sat waiting and listening tensely. When he heard the crash of several distant shots he sprang up from his seat and went to the street door, gun in hand. He waited, listening intently as the echoes of the shots faded and died. He fought against the impulse to leave the office to investigate, aware that the shooting could be a trick to draw him out into the open. He extinguished the lamp and stood to one side of the big front window, watching the approaches to the office.

Minutes passed slowly, dragging in the suspense of Starrett's ignorance of what was going on. His eyes were accustomed to the darkness but he could see nothing out front, and was startled when an unseen hand rattled the handle of the street door. He cocked his gun and waited, ready for action while concern for Spencer and Lunt unwound in his mind as he considered their continued absence.

They should have returned by now, and he feared that the shooting he heard had involved the two Circle B punchers.

A whispering of voices sounded outside and Starrett strained his ears to make sense of them.

'That Ranger has got to be inside!' The voice was so low it sounded like a hiss of expelled breath.

'He wouldn't be sitting in the dark if he's a Texas Ranger,' a second voice replied in a stronger tone. 'Step aside, Tricker, and I'll kick the door in. If there is anyone inside guarding the prisoners then I'll kill him. We've got to bust Satterfield out of here before anyone shows up from Circle B. From what you've told me I guess this is our only chance, and we've got to make the most of it.'

'Listen, Wyatt, you'll do more harm than good to Mr Satterfield's case by busting him loose,' Tricker protested. 'I know the ins and outs of the law, and there are better ways of handling this. If you kill a Ranger you'll have an army of those badge-toters in here before you could bury him. The Rangers always take care of their men.'

'Quit your gabbing and get the hell out of my way. I'm going through this door to get the boss out. I reckon this place is deserted. Maybe that Ranger heard the shooting a while back and took off — or he should have done if he had any sense. I reckon he's running for Circle B right now, with his tail between his legs. He was a fool to come in here alone and buck the whole town. It's a pity I didn't ride in with the RS crew, but I didn't know there was trouble here until I arrived. I've sent for the outfit, and they'll be riding in around sunup.'

Starrett recalled that a man named Wyatt was running Satterfield's RS ranch. He considered that the man was at present alone outside with the lawyer, and was tempted to open the street door and throw down on them. He needed time, and by taking the key men of Satterfield's organization out of circulation he would be buying himself some of that vital commodity. He reached out to unbolt the door but paused when Tricker said:

'It won't hurt to leave Satterfield behind bars until tomorrow. By then I should be able to arrange for him to be freed legally. It would be wrong for you to kill the Ranger inside town limits. Get him out of town to do the job and no one would ever learn what happened to him, but kill him here and the world will know about it.'

'Damn you and the law!' Wyatt snarled. 'Satterfield won't be too pleased if I leave him skulking in jail overnight. We'll do this my way. I need to talk to Satterfield mighty quick. That's why I came into town. There's hell busted loose on the range. I sent a dozen guns out from Cash's place this morning to hit Circle B hard and the whole damned bunch of them have been shot to hell.'

'Then this is more serious than I

reckoned,' Tricker replied angrily. 'I could see it was all getting out of hand. I've been telling Satterfield for weeks to pull in his horns around Circle B but he wouldn't listen to reason. Well, I'm not gonna stick around and wait for the law to start cleaning up. I'm getting the hell out of here while the going is good.'

'You ain't going anywhere,' Wyatt snarled. 'You've been drawing good pay for doing damn all, and now the going has got tough you want to up stakes and run. Well, you better think again, you little runt, or I'll gut-shoot you. Nobody is running out on this set-up unless the boss gives the word. Now get out of here before I lose my temper, and you better be around in the morning when Satterfield will really need you or I'll have the outfit hunt you down.'

Starrett heard boots scraping the hard ground as Tricker departed hurriedly. He reached out with his left hand, unbolted the street door, and then jerked it open wide. Wyatt was staring after the departing Tricker. Starrett cocked his pistol and Wyatt swung towards him when he heard the ominous clicks of the weapon, instinctively dropping his hand to the butt of his holstered gun.

'Try pulling that gun and you won't see the inside of this jail,' Starrett warned grimly. 'You'll be lying on the undertaker's slab being prepared for your funeral.'

Wyatt lifted his hands away from his waist and Starrett slugged him with the barrel of his pistol. Wyatt groaned and dropped. Starrett bent and delivered a second blow to the man's head. Wyatt relaxed noiselessly and Starrett relieved him of his holstered gun. He dragged Wyatt in clear of the door, closed and bolted it, then went to the desk and struck a match to light the lamp. When he turned to confront Wyatt he found the big man out cold. He holstered his pistol and manhandled him into the cells.

Millet came to the barred door of his

cell, gazed at the unconscious Wyatt, and muttered an epithet as he returned to his bunk. Starrett put the cell keys in his pocket when he left the office. He locked the outer door and went along the street, wanting to discover the fate of Spencer and Lunt.

The town was still very quiet as Starrett walked through the shadows. He saw a light in Vince Tricker's office, and peered through the window to see the lawyer at his desk; he was filling a leather satchel with papers. He entered the office to confront the man.

Tricker froze as his street door opened, and his angular face turned pale when he saw Starrett's ominous figure approaching him. He quickly jerked open the right-hand drawer of his desk and started to reach inside, but halted the action when Starrett drew his gun. He pulled his hand clear as if the drawer was the inside of a hot stove.

'If that's a gun you're after,' Starrett said sharply, 'then you better lift it slowly, and don't point it at me.'

Tricker lifted a pistol into view and dropped it on the desk. His lips moved as if in prayer but no sound emerged from his mouth. He gazed at Starrett and his expression showed exactly what was passing through his mind: desperation.

'Like Wyatt said, nobody runs out,' Starrett observed. 'You'll be needed to tell the law what has been going on around here and to point out the guilty men.'

'Where's Wyatt?' Tricker demanded.

'He's behind bars.' Starrett laughed harshly. 'He was so keen to get into the jail I decided to let him in. Now you can share a cell with him. I heard every incriminating word that passed between you two outside the jail, so come on, and don't make a fuss or it'll go hard with you.'

Tricker swallowed as if he were choking and emerged from behind the desk, but paused when Starrett did not move. The lawyer looked like a frightened rabbit as his gaze probed

Starrett's harsh face.

'What?' he demanded when Starrett remained silent and motionless.

'Several shots were fired just before you and Wyatt showed up at the jail, so tell me what happened,' Starrett said.

'It was Wyatt.' Tricker spoke in a rush, as if eager to get rid of the words. 'Two Circle B men came into the saloon for a drink and Wyatt braced them. He shot them when they reached for their guns.'

Starrett's eyes glinted. 'Are they dead?' he asked bleakly.

'I guess so. Wyatt is a killer!'

Starrett stepped aside and motioned with his pistol. Tricker sighed heavily. He left his office with Starrett at his back, and went to the jail with no thought of resisting.

As he unlocked the office door, Starrett heard the sound of hoofs along the street.

'You're in bad trouble now.' Tricker laughed in a relieved tone. 'That sounds like the RS outfit coming in. Wyatt is expecting them. They were due to show up before riding out to Circle B to finish the raid that was started this morning. Now we'll see what kind of a lawman you are, Ranger.'

Starrett thrust Tricker into the office and followed quickly. He slammed and bolted the door, grasped Tricker by the scruff of the neck, and hurried him into the cell block. Before the lawyer could catch his breath he was behind bars with the door locked. Starrett drew his pistol and went back into the office. If the RS outfit was coming then he had a real fight on his hands.

He blew out the lamp and went to the window. As he peered out into the darkness several shots blasted through the heavy silence and he saw orange muzzle-flame stabbing through nearby shadows. A rider dismounted heavily from a horse opposite the law office window and fired two quick shots at the gun flashes spouting at his rear. Two guns replied to his shooting as the man came running towards the darkened law office.

Starrett unbolted the office door, dragged it open, and stepped into the doorway with his pistol levelled. The approaching man suddenly dropped to one knee and twisted to face his attackers. Guns blasted raucously and slugs flew. Starrett had to hold his fire for he was unaware of the identity of those involved in the shooting. His ears were battered by the hammering guns. He stepped outside, to the right of the doorway, and awaited an opportunity to get into the fight.

Two figures showed up on the other side of the street, and gun flashes marked their position. The man in the street returned fire before rising and coming towards the office.

'Declare yourself!' Starrett called sharply, cocking his pistol. 'What's all the shooting about?'

'I'm Del Baker, a Texas Ranger!' was the reply, then his voice was drowned out by the two guns renewing fire at him.

Starrett lifted his gun instantly, his

mind reeling with shock. He began shooting at the two men across the street and his accurate fire drove them into cover. Starrett ran out to where Baker was kneeling and dragged the young Ranger to his feet. He continued to fire into the shadows across the street as he half-carried his sidekick into the law office.

'What's going on, Del?' Starrett demanded as he bolted the street door.

'All hell busted loose out at Circle B,' Baker replied. 'Joe Kenton turned up with word of what was happening here in town and I decided to come in and back you, but as I left the ranch a bunch of riders attacked from all sides. I was in the clear and made a run for town but two of the bunch chased after me. So what's happening around here? I'm ready to start handling my side of the business.'

'I've got this local business pretty well under control,' Starrett replied, and explained the incidents that had occurred. He checked the street outside as he spoke. Nothing was moving now and he eased away from the window. 'I reckon all we've got to do is hold on to what we've got and if we can get through to sunup then we'll be on the winning side.'

'That's pretty good going,' Baker enthused, 'and the trouble is boiling up out at Circle B. Bellamy returned from town and told me about Don Emilio and his son. They had worked out a plan that would bring Ramirez into the open where their combined outfits could force a showdown. Bellamy is going to gather a sizeable herd in his home pasture as bait to pull in Ramirez, and Don Emilio and his crew will ambush the rustlers if they fall for the trick.'

Starrett shook his head doubtfully. 'I hope Bellamy knows what he's doing,' he mused. 'Those Mexicans are real tricky. If Don Emilio is playing it straight then OK, it might spell the end of Ramirez and his crew, but Bellamy is taking a long chance, and if Don Emilio is gambling on some crooked plan of his own then Circle B could lose out all round. I guess Bellamy is a gambling man, and he's betting all or nothing.'

'Do you reckon Don Emilio isn't on the level?' Baker demanded.

'I don't know what to think, but the next few hours will be critical for all of us.' Starrett shook his head as he considered, and then ducked as a spate of shooting erupted outside. The big front window of the office shattered into a hundred pieces under the hammer blows of questing lead. Starrett flung himself at Baker and took him to the floor in a desperate attempt to escape the fusillade.

10

The shooting seemed to go on for ever. Bullets slammed into the office from at least five guns and flailed through the darkness in a haphazard search for targets. The drum-roll fire of shooting hammered and echoed around the street as the attack continued unabated. Slugs smacked into woodwork and tore out splinters and slivers. The iron stove clanged like an anvil as bullets struck it in their blind flight. The street door suddenly swung open when the bolt was shattered, and Starrett lifted his pistol to cover the threat of being overrun. His ears protested at the overwhelming thunder which assailed them, and he winced when a ricocheting slug slashed across his left cheek like a flash of lightning.

An indistinct figure suddenly appeared in the open doorway and a gun flashed.

A slug crackled between Starrett and Baker and they fired in unison. The figure was blasted away as if struck by a giant hand. Starrett moved to the left side of the doorway to cover the street, and began shooting at the gun flashes splitting the shadows opposite. The attack was cut off suddenly and an uneasy silence settled. The stinking reek of gun-smoke was strong in the dark air.

'Those two who followed me from Circle B must have gathered a few friends to side them,' Baker observed.

'There are a lot of men in town who carry guns for Satterfield,' Starrett replied, reloading the empty chambers in his pistol.

'Hey, you in the law office,' a voice called echoingly from across the street. 'Turn Satterfield loose, if you know what's good for you. There'll be twenty or more of us out here in a few minutes, so you better get the hell out before we come in and get you.'

'Sounds like a stand-off to me,' Starrett shouted in reply. 'The minute you look like busting in here I'm gonna shoot Satterfield. I know he's guilty of murder, among other things, and he won't live to see daylight if you keep this up. He sure as hell won't want you to come in here if it means he'll cash his chips. I'll get him to tell you what he wants, if you've got any doubt. But I guess you can work it out for yourselves what he would tell you right now so pull out and leave us in peace.'

'Bluffing won't get you off the hook,' the anonymous voice replied. 'I never heard of a lawman shooting his prisoners, so cut out the guff and turn Satterfield loose.'

Starrett lifted his pistol and fired a shot into the shadows opposite. There was no reply and echoes began to fade.

'You've given them something to think about,' Baker observed. 'Do you think it will hold them off until sunup?'

'It has given them doubts, and that's all to the good.' Starrett eased back from the street door. 'I don't think they can overrun us, so all we've got to do is sit tight until daylight. But I'd sure like to be in two places at once.'

'Here, and out at Circle B, huh?' Baker laughed drily. 'Yeah, I'm wondering what's going on with Bellamy.' He stifled a groan of pain as he shifted position. 'So we've got a long night ahead of us and no chance of help coming from anywhere. This will teach me a lot about law dealing in the raw, huh?'

'This is all it is ever about,' Starrett replied. 'We locate the bad men and put them out of business with hot lead. If they resist we fight until they or we are dead.'

The silence seemed intolerable after the shooting, and Starrett's ears were ringing from the shock of the shots. He warned Baker that he was about to move and then got to his feet and crossed to the window to look out at the street in front of the law office. He stayed low while he watched and listened, and compressed his lips when he caught the distant sound of approaching hoofs.

'I thought I heard riders coming, Del,' he said. 'Sounds like a lot of them too. You better stand by. It can only be some more of Satterfield's men. This looks like turning into the mother and father of all fights! There are some boxes of spare cartridges on the desk. You better load up and get ready to defend yourself. These men won't even try to take us prisoner. They'll come in here stomping, and it'll be us underfoot.'

'I'm ready for them,' Baker replied grimly. 'If we've got enough cartridges to do the job then let them all come!'

'That's the spirit.' Starrett moved across the office and broken glass crunched under his boots. He took a Winchester from the rack on the wall behind the desk, feeling every inch of the way through the darkness, then he moved back to the window. The group of riders was closer now. He jacked a shell into the breech of the rifle and raised the long gun to cover the street. The sound of hoofs stopped abruptly, and Starrett could imagine the riders dismounting and sneaking forward on foot. His pulses were racing; his heart beating faster than normal. He caught sight of a short, blocky figure easing forward from the right, and covered it with the rifle, his finger curved around the trigger.

'That's near enough!' he shouted at length. The figure halted abruptly. 'Who are you and what do you want?'

'This is Sheriff Brady from Birchwood,' was the reply. 'I got a report today from a Circle B rider that there is trouble here so I've brought a posse along. I was told a Texas Ranger had come into town to clean up, so tell me who you are.'

'I'm Buck Starrett, Texas Ranger! OK, Sheriff, come in alone so I can check you out.'

The sheriff came forward slowly, his hands held away from his sides. He approached the law office, starlight glinting on the law badge on his shirt front. Starrett stepped into the doorway with his rifle pointing at the lawman's ample stomach. The sheriff halted, hitched up his sagging gun belt, and spread his hands wide. His breathing was ragged, his voice wheezy when he spoke.

'Where in hell is Rafe Millet?' he demanded. 'He's supposed to be running things around here.'

'He's behind bars, where he should have been a long time ago.' Starrett glanced over his shoulder. 'Del, light the lamp, if it still works.'

Baker complied and yellow light flared in the office. Starrett inspected the sheriff, a short, fleshy man past middle age. The buckle of Brady's gun belt was almost hidden by the overhanging cliff of his paunch, and the belt sagged to his right to hold the holstered pistol under his right hand. His beady eyes studied Starrett's ominous figure and he nodded slowly.

'So what's been going on?' he demanded. 'It seems quiet enough right now. Have I had this long ride for nothing?'

Starrett was wondering whether Brady was also on Satterfield's payroll. He was on his guard as he explained what had occurred in town since his arrival. Brady listened impassively, his fleshy lips pulled into a thin, uncompromising line. His dark eyes glinted under the low-pulled brim of his Stetson.

'Millett is a renegade, huh?' he demanded at length. 'Heck, I always had my suspicions, but no one ever complained about him. I was the deputy here before Satterfield took over, and he was a hard-working businessman in those days. So he turned sour, huh? OK, I'll look into this business. I'll stop the rot and put the town back to rights. Give me the keys to the cells. I want to talk to Satterfield. You reckon you got some witnesses to back up your actions?'

'Sure.' Starrett handed over the bunch of keys and Brady checked them.

'I'll call in my posse now.' Brady turned to the door and yelled into the darkness. 'Hey, Luke, bring the posse in. Tell them to be on their guard, although everything looks to be under control here.' He glanced at Starrett. 'Is there anyone else around you figure should be behind bars?'

'There are several,' Starrett replied, 'but so long as we hold Satterfield it doesn't matter about the rest. We can pick them up any time.'

Brady nodded, Starrett heard boots approaching the street door. A tall, thin man wearing a deputy sheriff's badge and holding a pistol in his right hand appeared in the doorway.

'Luke Thompson,' Brady introduced. 'I'll put him in here as the local deputy. 'Luke, Millett is behind bars. You got the job of handling the law around here as of this moment. This is Starrett, a Texas Ranger. From what he says the trouble around here is just about finished. We'll work with him to straighten out the town. OK, so let's take a look at our prisoners and get to it.'

Brady approached the door between the office and the cells and inserted a key into the lock. Starrett remained in the background, content to let the county law take over. He was impatient now to get out to Circle B to check on the situation there. Brady jerked open the door and stepped into the cell block.

'Get a lamp in here, Luke,' Brady ordered, pausing in the doorway.

Starrett lowered his rifle and put it down on the desk. He motioned for Baker to holster his pistol. Baker was looking pale and strained but he grinned at Starrett.

Luke Thompson put a match to a wall-mounted lamp on the back wall and then lifted the lamp from its bracket. He pushed by Brady and entered the cells, followed closely by the sheriff. The jail was rocked instantly by several blasting shots. Starrett jerked his pistol from its holster in an instinctive reaction. The shooting was inside the cell block, and for a moment he thought Brady was shooting the prisoners. Then he saw the sheriff pitch to the floor, riddled with bullets, blood spurting from his throat.

Starrett flattened himself against the wall beside the door, thrust his gun hand around the door jamb, and triggered three shots into the cell from which gun flashes were erupting. He heard a terrific crash from inside the cell block and dropped to the floor to squirm into the doorway at ground level. Luke Thompson had managed to put the lamp he was carrying on a table before taking a slug, and its yellow light illuminated the grim scene inside the cells. Trig Wyatt was down on one knee at the door of his cell, holding a smoking .45 in his right hand.

The rear wall in the cell occupied by Satterfield had a barred window in it, and Starrett saw that the window and part of the wall had been torn out. There was no sign of Satterfield. Starrett drew a bead on Wyatt and squeezed his trigger. The bullet struck the RS foreman in the chest. Wyatt went over on his back and relaxed. Gun smoke drifted thickly through the cells.

Rafe Millett was lying on the floor of his cell. He was unharmed, his glinting eyes watching Starrett, who got to his feet and moved into the cell block with Baker crowding him from behind.

'They've busted Satterfield out through the back wall,' Baker declared.

'Sure.' Millett got to his feet, grinning. 'One of Satterfield's friends passed a couple of guns through that back window a while back. Wyatt got one and Satterfield kept the other. They waited for that door to open before starting their play by roping the bars in the window of Satterfield's cell and dragging them out with a couple of horses. You were expected to walk in, Ranger, but Brady got the dirty job, huh? So Satterfield has escaped, but he'll be back, you can bet, and then the rest of us will be walking out of here. You can't win against the whole town, mister.'

Starrett bent over Luke Thompson. The deputy was alive, but bleeding profusely from a shoulder wound.

'Del, you stick around here and start cleaning up with the posse,' Starrett said. 'I want to get after Satterfield.'

'I can handle this!' Baker replied.

Starrett went back into the front office. Half a dozen posse men were crowding in from the street with guns drawn. Starrett explained what had occurred. The men from Birchwood were shocked by the news of the sheriff's death.

'I need to borrow a horse,' Starrett said. 'I'm going after Satterfield and whoever busted him out of jail.'

'Take Brady's horse,' one of the posse men replied. 'He won't need it any more.'

Starrett hurried out to the street with the posse man following him.

'That big dun is Brady's mount,' the man said.

Starrett ran to the dun and vaulted into the saddle. He swung the animal and rode along the street to the right until he reached the livery barn, then hammered through the shadows to the back lots. He reined in and listened intently. When he heard the faint sound of receding hoofs in the distance he sent the dun in pursuit. Satterfield was out on the trail, and probably heading for his ranch.

The dun travelled fast and Starrett kept reining in to listen for distant hoofbeats. He estimated that three horses were ahead of him. He followed grimly. He had no idea where the RS ranch was situated, and he urged the dun on to greater effort, determined to ride down his quarry.

Starlight aided him as he rode. The night sky was streaked with silver light although he could not see the moon. His senses were keen and he rode as if on a knife edge, eyes narrowed and ears strained. An hour passed and he could still hear the sound of hoofs ahead. He pushed on, aware that he had to take Satterfield in order to bring about a successful conclusion to his assignment.

When he reined in yet again to listen

for hoof beats there was only intense silence pressing against his ears. He remained motionless while tense moments slipped by. He gripped his reins with hands clenched in frustration when he realized that Satterfield had stopped riding. Perhaps the big man was waiting in ambush. Starrett clenched his teeth and urged the dun on at a walk. He was not ready to give up the trail, and if his quarry had turned at bay then so much the better.

A night breeze was blowing directly into his face, and Starrett canted his head in order to catch any sound ahead. He heard distant hoofs for a moment, sounding mockingly close in the half-darkness, then they stopped before he could get a fix on their direction. He drew his pistol and held it ready as he went on slowly. Then he heard a flurry of rapidly receding hoof beats somewhere in the night. He guessed Satterfield was making a run for it.

The dun was standing with its head lowered. Starrett kicked his heels against its flanks. The horse hit a gallop in a few strides, but Starrett slowed the animal instantly, aware that it was madness to ride so fast across the darkened range. All it needed to bring disaster was a hoof in a gopher hole.

He reined in again to listen for sound, canting his head as he turned it to the left and then to the right, his ears strained for the tell-tale beat of hoofs. He heard nothing but the sighing of the breeze. He waited patiently, aware that Satterfield was playing a cat-and-mouse game. Moments later he caught a faint sound but it seemed to be to his left and he frowned as he eased around to face the new direction. He drew his pistol and cocked it.

The dun refused to move when Starrett used his heels, and he peered into the surrounding shadows. The horse was Sheriff Brady's and not accustomed to Starrett's style of riding. The animal was gazing into the night, its ears forward, and Starrett knew enough about horses to accept that it was aware of someone ahead in the darkness. A moment later he caught the sound of a number of horses approaching from the left. He lifted his gun, ready to sell his life dearly if the newcomers should prove to be friends of Satterfield.

A horse whinnied and the bay answered instantly. Starrett narrowed his eyes as he attempted to pierce the gloom, and when at last he saw movement he called urgently.

'This is Texas Ranger Buck Starrett. Declare yourselves!'

'Starrett, this is Joe Kenton, livery-man of Adobe Flat. I'm on my way back to town with a couple of Circle B riders. What in hell are you doing out here?'

Three riders took shape and reined up in front of Starrett, who explained the situation. Kenton whistled softly in surprise, and then laughed.

'Toke Bellamy has had better luck than you,' he reported. 'Ramirez made another attempt to run off that herd at Circle B and walked into a trap. Don

Emilio was watching from Mexico, and as soon as Ramirez crossed the river Alvarez's outfit followed and hit Ramirez and his rustlers from behind. I arrived at Circle B as the battle ended, and counted more than twenty dead rustlers, Ramirez among them. Don Emilio's men sure didn't take any prisoners. I guess there won't be any more rustling in these parts if you can take Satterfield again.'

'I'm on my way to pick him up right now,' Starrett said.

'I'll ride with you — show you the way to RS,' Kenton decided. 'Sam, Hank,' he addressed the two riders accompanying him, 'ride into town and help that posse keep order until we come back with Satterfield.'

The two men rode off in the direction of Adobe Flat. Starrett heaved a sigh as he considered the situation.

'I need to get to RS fast, Joe. But how do you feel about going up against Satterfield?'

'The law comes first,' Kenton replied.

'Over the years Satterfield has robbed and murdered his way to the top, and it's time he was taken down.'

'You got proof of your accusations?' Starrett demanded.

'I sure have!' Kenton spurred his horse. 'I thought you said you were in a hurry!'

Starrett rode in beside the liveryman. There was no need to listen for hoof-beats now. They travelled at a steady clip, and Starrett reloaded his pistol in anticipation of a showdown. Kenton pushed on fast, seemingly determined to bring his crooked brother-in-law to his just deserts.

Later, a square of yellow light piercing the darkness ahead gave Starrett a hint that he was nearing the RS ranch. Kenton slackened speed, and when he spoke his voice was distorted by an eager passion.

'That's RS ahead,' he warned. 'Looks like Satterfield went home. I'm wondering how many of his outfit are around. There were several stretched out dead at Circle B. They were there helping

Ramirez run off the herd. Satterfield has had his grimy fingers in all the crooked pies cooked up around here.'

'Let us sneak in and take him by surprise,' Starrett suggested. 'Will his wife be at the ranch?'

'The hell she is! Mary left Satterfield last year — had her fill of him by then.'

They dismounted out of earshot of the ranch and walked in silently. Starrett held his pistol ready. When he could see the dark pile of a low building ahead he reached out, grasped Kenton's arm, and whispered:

'We'd better not walk straight in, Joe. I'd like to take a look around first. You stay out here while I go ahead.'

'You don't know how many men are around,' Kenton replied, 'but I guess you know your business. I'll cover your back from the edge of the porch. Give a shout if you need to come out the front door.'

Starrett slid away to the right. He circled the house and moved through dense shadows looking for the back door. He found it standing open and, as he considered entering the intense blackness of the kitchen, a horse whinnied somewhere close by, invisible in the gloom. Starrett paused against the back wall, listening intently for other sounds. He stepped back into the doorway of the house, and froze when a hard object was rammed into his right side with painful force. Then a hand came out of the darkness and grasped his gun hand, trapping his trigger finger against the cylinder of the pistol so that he was unable to fire the weapon. A heavy figure crowded him and a knee came slamming into his groin.

Starrett twisted to his right. As the pistol boring into his side slid away it exploded with a blasting crash and orange gun flame tore through the darkness. Starrett smelled gun smoke but the bullet did not touch his flesh. He smashed his head forward in a vicious butt and made contact with his assailant's face. The hand grasping his gun hand fell away. The man uttered a cry of pain and faded into the shadows. Starrett hurled himself to the floor, his pistol lifting. He landed on his left side, gun hand swinging, and fired when he caught a glimpse of his assailant silhouetted in the open doorway.

The man uttered a thin cry of agony as he was hurled backwards out of the doorway by the impact of the bullet. Starrett blinked rapidly, his eyes momentarily dazzled by gun flame. He rolled to his left, fetched up against a table leg, and surged to his feet. He leaned against an inner wall and moved along it as gun echoes faded, his left hand feeling for an interior door to gain access to the front of the house.

At that moment a door along a passage was opened and a shaft of lamplight sprang into being. Starrett peered out of the kitchen and saw the big figure of Red Satterfield emerging from a room on the left, carrying a pair of saddlebags. Satterfield hurried towards the front door.

'Hold it, Satterfield,' Starrett called.

'You ain't going anywhere except back to jail.'

Satterfield halted as if he had run into a wall. He glanced back over his shoulder, gazed at Starrett's big figure and levelled gun, and dropped his right hand to his gunbelt.

Starrett fired without seeming to aim. His bullet smashed into Satterfield's holster, clanging against the pistol inside it. The impact thrust Satterfield half-around and he dropped the saddlebags as he swung back to face Starrett, who waited with levelled gun.

'The next one will be dead centre,' Starrett called. 'You better put your hands up while you're still breathing.'

'You're not taking me back to jail,' Satterfield snarled.

'So pull your gun,' Starrett said harshly.

'You won't shoot me,' Satterfield declared. 'You want me alive.'

'But I don't care one way or the other, Red,' Joe Kenton said from the shadows surrounding the front door. 'I'd like the chance to put a slug into your crooked hide. Don't turn around. Just put your hands up.'

Satterfield's face took on a hunted expression. He half-turned his head to look over his shoulder in the direction of Kenton's voice, then decided against it. He lifted his hands slowly.

'OK, you got me cold,' he said softly. 'But it's a long way back to town.'

Starrett smiled as he went forward and relieved Satterfield of his gun. Kenton came forward.

'I ought to shoot you out of hand, Red,' the liveryman declared, 'but you'll have a fair trial before they hang you. I got the deadwood on you — been storing evidence for years, and now the law is back in Adobe Flat I can wait to see you get what is coming to you. Let's get him back to jail as fast as we can, Starrett.'

'Not so fast.' Starrett shook his head. 'Go check Brady's saddlebags on the dun for handcuffs and we'll make Satterfield comfortable. With him under arrest this business is finished, and I need to rustle up some grub before anything else.'

'You take care of Satterfield and I'll see to the grub,' Kenton replied with a grin.

Starrett nodded. He could feel his mind slipping down from the high pinnacle of alertness and determination that always gripped him when on an assignment, and he became aware of how good it felt to act like a human being again.

THE END

We do hope that you have enjoyed reading this large print book.

Did you know that all of our titles are available for purchase?

We publish a wide range of high quality large print books including:
Romances, Mysteries, Classics
General Fiction
Non Fiction and Westerns

Special interest titles available in large print are:
The Little Oxford Dictionary
Music Book, Song Book
Hymn Book, Service Book

Also available from us courtesy of Oxford University Press:
Young Readers' Dictionary
(large print edition)
Young Readers' Thesaurus
(large print edition)

For further information or a free brochure, please contact us at:
Ulverscroft Large Print Books Ltd.,
The Green, Bradgate Road, Anstey,
Leicester, LE7 7FU, England.
Tel: (00 44) **0116 236 4325**
Fax: (00 44) **0116 234 0205**